THE VAMPIRE SERPENT

SHERLOCK HOLMES' TALES OF TERROR

THE VAMPIRE SERPENT

Kel Richards

Based on characters created by
Sir Arthur Conan Doyle

BEACON BOOK

A Beacon Book

First published in Australia in 1997 by
Beacon Communications Pty Ltd
PO Box 1317, Lane Cove NSW 2066

Copyright © Beacon Communications 1997

National Library of Australia
Cataloguing-in-Publication data
I. Doyle, Arthur Conan, Sir, 1859-1930
II Title. (Series: Sherlock Holmes Tales of Terror)
A823.3

ISBN 0 9587020 2 0

Typeset by Beacon Communications, Sydney
Printed in Australia by Australian Print Group

Cover art Philip Cornell
Cover design Graham Wye

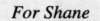

For Shane

THE VAMPIRE SERPENT

1

'Mr Holmes! Dr Watson! Come quickly,' shouted the visitor who burst into our rooms at 221B Baker Street. Holmes and I looked up from our breakfast table to discover that our early morning visitor was the Reverend Henry Bunyan, the vicar of our local parish church, St Bede's of Baker Street. Mr Bunyan was a middle-aged man, portly and affable—a descendant of the famous author of *Pilgrim's Progress*—and something of an expert on folklore.

He stood trembling in our doorway, his face flushed and his manner agitated.

'Come,' said Sherlock Holmes, springing out of his chair. 'Come in and take a seat. Tell us what has happened.'

'There is no time for that, Mr Holmes,' said the clergyman, twisting his broad-brimmed black hat in his hands, 'You must come at once. It's my neighbour, Crosby, the banker. He's dead, Mr Holmes. It's hideous, utterly hideous.'

Without a word Holmes reached for his jacket. As

he slipped it on he said, 'Come along, Watson—the game's afoot, and I shall want you at my side.'

As I swallowed a piece of toast and reached for my coat, Mr Bunyan said, 'Oh, yes Dr Watson—your medical knowledge will be needed.'

We followed the bustling, agitated clergyman down our stairs and out into the early morning mist. It was a cold, gray, overcast day. As we walked briskly down the street, Mr Bunyan explained breathlessly, 'Mrs Crosby came to me first thing this morning saying that her husband had not been home all night. He had given her no warning that he would be away, and as he is normally the most considerate and reliable of men, she was deeply alarmed, and asked me what should be done. I proposed searching the bank premises and the surrounding area, which we did. We found poor Crosby—or, rather, what is left of him—in an alley behind the bank.'

By the time Mr Bunyan had completed his explanations we had walked rapidly passed the parish church of St Bede's, and the vicarage next door, and reached the two-storey brick building which consisted of bank offices downstairs, and accommodation for the manager upstairs. Here the morning mist seemed to have accumulated in cold, clammy white tentacles that wrapped themselves around us. Bunyan led us down the narrow pedestrian lane between the vicarage and the bank, and then turned into the even narrower dark alley that ran behind the back wall of the bank building.

Lying against this wall was something covered by a sheet of canvas.

2

'I covered him up, as you can see,' said Bunyan. 'It seemed the decent thing to do.'

Holmes stepped forward and pulled back the canvas revealing one of the most horrible sights I have ever encountered. It was a dead body all right, but it was a withered and shrunken dead body. The skin was clinging to the bones like dried parchment. The body looked as if it had been sucked dry. The mouth was frozen open in a silent scream of terror.

'Are you certain this is Crosby?' asked Holmes.

'Who else could it be?' replied the vicar. 'Look at that red hair and moustache. And he's wearing the clothes Crosby was wearing when his wife last saw him. But, I grant you the body has been so horribly treated that his face is impossible to recognise.'

'How old was Crosby?'

'In his early forties. He has had a very rapid rise in the bank to have become a manager at such an early age. His wife, or, I should say, his widow, is a great deal younger than himself—she is barely nineteen.'

'This is indeed remarkable,' said Sherlock Holmes as he dropped down on one knee to examine the corpse. 'What do you make of this, Watson?'

I conducted a brief examination. 'Astonishing! There is no blood in this body. It has been drained of every last drop of blood.'

Glancing down the alley, Holmes spotted a street urchin he recognised.

'Wiggins! Come here a moment!'

'Yes, Mr Holmes,' panted the grubby faced little scoundrel as he ran towards us, 'What'd you want?'

'Here's sixpence—run and fetch a policeman. Urgently!'

'Yes, Mr Holmes. If you wants a bobby—I'll find you a bobby.' And with that he sprinted away.

'He's as sharp as a needle, and totally reliable, that one,' said Holmes, nodding in the direction of the rapidly disappearing figure. 'Now, Mr Bunyan—when was Mr Crosby last seen alive?'

'At supper last night,' replied the clergyman. 'Mrs Crosby told me that she ate supper with her husband at about eight o'clock.'

'And after that . . .?'

'He said he had some urgent work to finish, and went downstairs to his office in the bank chambers.'

'So,' muttered Holmes thoughtfully, 'he was alive shortly after eight o'clock last night. Watson, what would you say was the cause of death?'

'I've never seen a body in this condition before, Holmes—never. That makes it extremely difficult to answer your question. But as a guess—and it's only a guess—I would say that he died from the loss of blood. Of course, he may already have been dead at the time the blood was drained from his body, but there is no obvious wound or sign of assault.'

'You confirm my own observations, Watson.'

Sherlock Holmes took a magnifying lens from his coat pocket and began a closer examination of the corpse. 'Aha!' he cried triumphantly, after several minutes had passed. 'There is a wound, Watson—admittedly a very small one—here upon the neck. Here, take my lens and see for yourself.'

Through the lens I could make out a small, round incision, smeared with dried, blackened blood. 'Remarkable,' I said. 'I've never seen anything like it.'

'Neither have I,' admitted Holmes. 'We are facing here an entirely new horror. The man or creature who did this to poor Crosby kills in a way I have never encountered before.'

'I have!' exclaimed Henry Bunyan. 'At least—in my readings in folklore I have come upon a creature capable of inflicting just such an injury, and causing just such a death.'

Holmes turned and looked at the clergyman, asking a question by raising an eyebrow as he did so.

'A vampire, Mr Holmes—a vampire! There are vampires in the folk tales of many countries, but especially eastern Europe and the Balkans; countries such as Albania, Hungary, and Romania. Can all these stories be mere superstition? Or is there something behind them? The state of poor Crosby's corpse seem to tell us that the folk tales are true—and that a vampire is now stalking the streets and back alleys of London.'

2

The Reverend Henry Bunyan's remark about vampires left Holmes and myself rather lost for words. However, we were saved from the need to reply by the arrival of Constable Barrett.

'Morning Mr Holmes, Dr Watson. Morning Vicar. Young Wiggins told me you wanted to see me.'

'We want you to see *this*,' said Holmes, stepping aside and showing the policeman the corpse.

'Great heavens!' cried Barrett. 'What a horrible way to die! What is this, Mr Holmes?'

'Murder, Barrett—foul murder. I would be very pleased if you would summon assistance and inform Scotland Yard at once.'

'I shall, Mr Holmes—immediately.'

As the constable departed, Holmes began examining the ground around the corpse.

'Any useful marks have been trampled over and scuffed up,' he said, after a minute's study.

'That would have been Mrs Crosby and myself,'

said Bunyan. 'I'm sorry about that, Mr Holmes.'

'Regrettable, but unavoidable,' muttered Holmes. 'It would have been useful if . . . hello, what's this?'

Following Holmes' pointing finger I saw a most unusual trail in the dust of that dark alley. It was a long, thin, sinuous winding trail— almost as if a heavy hose or pipe had been dragged through the dust.

'What on earth could have made such a mark?' I asked.

'At this stage, Watson, I haven't the faintest idea,' said Holmes, taking out his notebook and making a rapid sketch of the trail, 'and it may have nothing to do with Crosby's death, but at this point in the investigation everything must be checked. Bunyan, how did Mrs Crosby react to the discovery of her husband's body?'

'She collapsed, Mr Holmes,' replied the clergyman. 'Fainted dead away. As soon as she recovered I took her upstairs to her rooms, where she lay down on the settee. I had to leave her there in some distress in order to run and fetch you, Mr Holmes. In fact, I wonder, Dr Watson, whether you would be so good as to look in on Mrs Crosby and see how she is?'

'Yes, yes, of course,' I said, 'if you will just show me the way.'

Mr Bunyan led me back down the lane that separated the bank from his own residence, and indicated a door in the side of the bank building. Beside the door was a painted sign reading: 'Cox and Co. Bankers.' The vicar opened the door, which led to a short corridor beyond. The corridor ended in a door on one side, apparently leading into the bank chambers, and a flight of stairs on the other. Bunyan led the way up the stairs.

'It's me, Mrs Crosby—Henry Bunyan. I've brought a doctor with me,' he called out as we reached the top.

In any other circumstances the banker's wife would have been a remarkably pretty young woman, in fact, barely more than a girl. But when I saw her, her eyes were red and her face stained with tears. I checked her blood pressure and heart-rate and prescribed a mild sedative. Then, while Mr Bunyan went to find a neighbour who could sit with her, I returned to the dark alley where the corpse lay.

I discovered that Sherlock Holmes had been joined by several uniformed policemen, and by a stern-faced man in a gray suit and a bowler hat, whom I recognised as Inspector Lestrade of Scotland Yard.

'This is a bad business, Dr Watson,' he said grimly, as I joined the group. 'I was just explaining to Mr Holmes that this is the second murder of this type, in two days.'

'The second?'

'Indeed. The first was a Chinese sailor. His body was found near the docks around Limehouse. And it was just like this—a withered and shrunken corpse.'

'Drained of blood?' I asked.

'Every last drop of blood,' said Lestrade, nodding in agreement.

'Well, Holmes—how do you explain it?' I asked.

'I can't, Watson. At this moment I'm as baffled as you are. However, it does occur to me that if a new, and horrible method of murder has been developed, then the man most likely to be behind it is the fiendish Doctor Defoe.'

'I'm interested to hear you say that, Mr Holmes, for the same thought had crossed my own mind,' remarked Lestrade.

I turned up my collar against a light, misty rain that had begun to fall, carried by a chill wind. As I did so I asked, 'Who is this Doctor Defoe?'

'Let's return to the warmth and comfort of our rooms,' suggested Holmes, 'You too, Lestrade—and we'll talk about that evil man and the steps that can be taken against him.'

A short while later the three of us were gathered around a blazing log fire in our Baker Street rooms, with a tray of Mrs Hudson's tea and hot scones in front of us.

'Now, would one of you please explain,' I said, as I poured myself a cup of hot tea, 'just who this Doctor Defoe person is.'

'Dr Grimsby Defoe,' said Holmes, 'is the son of an Egyptian noblewoman—a descendent of the Pharaohs—and a Scottish engineer, who was working in Egypt when the two met. He has a brilliant mind and a twisted soul. I encountered him in the Limehouse kidnapping case. In that matter I succeeded in releasing his victims, but the man himself slipped through my net.'

'He now has control,' added Lestrade, 'of much of the old criminal network created by Professor Moriarty and Colonel Sebastian Moran.'

'What is he like?' I asked.

'Imagine,' replied Holmes, 'imagine a person—tall, lean and feline; high-shouldered, with a brow like Shakespeare and a face like Satan: a close-shaven skull, a short black beard and long magnetic eyes of the true cat green. Invest him with cruel cunning and a giant intellect; with all the resources of science, past and present, and with the resources of enormous wealth. Imagine that malevolent being and you have a mental picture of evil incarnate in one man—the fiendish Doctor Grimsby Defoe.'

Sherlock Holmes spoke with a cool determination, and I could see that thwarting the plans of Doctor Defoe was a matter of the utmost importance to him.

'I can add,' said Inspector Lestrade, as a he buttered a scone, 'that the police forces of every major city of the world are looking for him. None have ever succeeded in catching him. He is an elusive blighter, and if he really is the one behind these vampire murders, then the outlook is black—very black, indeed.'

While Sherlock Holmes, Inspector Lestrade and myself were conversing in our Baker Street rooms, other events were happening elsewhere, of which I learned only later.

Mrs Catherine Crosby lay upon her bed, moaning slightly as she tossed and turned in a restless sleep. Sitting by the side of her bed, knitting as she kept watch, was the Reverend Henry Bunyan's housekeeper—Mrs Newbigin. The only sound was the loud ticking of a grandfather clock in the hallway.

Mrs Newbigin walked over to the bed, and looking at the sleeping figure of Catherine Crosby. 'Poor thing. And so young too,' she murmured to herself. Then she returned to her chair and began counting stitches.

Thus occupied she failed to notice a strange, green mist that billowed in under the door of the bedroom. Having finished counting, she resumed her knitting.

But within a few minutes she notice how warm she was feeling. 'It's such a cold, bleak day outside,' she said to herself, 'I must be getting hot flushes.' A short while later she began to feel sleepy. She struggled to keep her eyelids open, but before long she was sound asleep.

As she began to snore the green mist stopped flowing across the floor of the bedroom, and the door opened. In stepped a tall, lean man, dressed in a dark suit and black cape. His skull was closely shaven, and he had a short, black beard. With him were two assistants—one small and quick, the other large, solid and slow moving. The small assistant checked the sleeping housekeeper and nodded to his master.

The man in the black cape moved up to the side of the bed, and stood looking down on the young, helpless, sleeping figure. He began to speak, in a voice that was little more than a whisper, but which was strangely commanding.

'Listen to me. Listen to me. You will hear nothing but the sound of my voice. Only the sound of my voice and nothing else. And you will believe and obey everything I tell you. Listen to me. Listen to me.'

The young widow turned restlessly in her sleep, and moaned softly.

'Now,' commanded the man in the black cape, 'you will open your eyes.'

The girl's eyes flickered open. She saw the tall man standing beside her bed and wanted to scream, but found herself completely unable to. She found her eyes drawn into his magnetic green eyes. She couldn't look away. It was as if she was falling into those eyes, drowning in a lake of green fire.

'Your husband had something that belonged to me,' said the insistent, masterful, whispering voice. 'He refused to return it to me, and now he has paid the ultimate penalty. Where is it?'

'I . . . don't . . . know,' came the feeble voice of the young woman in the bed.

'Is she telling the truth, master?' asked the small assistant.

'Yes. Under this control she would be incapable of lying to me.'

As Catherine Crosby lay, frozen with fear, unable to move, the green eyes of the man beside her bed seemed to glow with an unearthly light. He spoke again, this time in a whisper so quiet that she couldn't make out the words. They were strange words, perhaps foreign words. It sounded like some sort of chanting. As she listened to these sounds, the visitor beside her bed appeared—to her eyes—to change shape. His tall, black figure took on a writhing, sinuous, snake-like appearance. Within minutes it looked to Catherine as though a giant cobra was looming over her bed, ready to strike. She had never felt more terrified in her life. Then the cobra spoke to her, giving her instructions that she knew she would obey—that she would find it quite impossible to disobey. And then she fell into a deep black, well of sleep.

Half an hour later, Catherine Crosby drifted into wakefulness. She blinked and said, 'Are you still here, Mrs Newbigin?'

'Yes, dear,' said the old housekeeper, looking up from her knitting. 'How are you feeling?'

'I've just had the strangest dream—stranger than I could ever describe.'

'Perhaps it's the weather. I even nodded off for a little while myself. Now, how about a nice cup of tea?'

While this was happening upstairs, downstairs in the bank, the Chief Accountant, Robert Stine, was distracted with worry as he tried to keep the bank functioning efficiently without a manager. He had sent a messenger to the head office of Cox and Co. informing them of the tragedy, and asking that a relieving manager be sent as soon as possible.

Stine was sitting at Crosby's desk, sorting through the former manager's papers when he heard a noise and looked up. He was startled to see a tall, lean man, wearing a dark suit and a black cloak, standing on the other side of the desk.

'Who are you?' stammered Stine, indignantly, 'and how did you get in here. My clerk should have told you . . .'

'Your clerk understood how important it is that I see you,' said the stranger, in a quiet, commanding voice. 'He was very helpful in showing me in here. And now, you too will help me.'

The stranger had powerful, green eyes. Stine found it impossible to look away from those eyes.

14

Those eyes, and that voice! Robert Stine found himself saying, 'Yes, I'll help you. What can I do for you?' even though that was not what he had intended to say.

'Your late manager, Mr Crosby, had some property of mine. I believe he locked it in the bank vault. You will open the vault and return my property to me.'

'Yes . . . I will open the vault . . . return your property to you,' murmured Stine, rising from his desk, and moving, like a man in a dream, towards the strongroom.

A moment later the two men stood before a heavy, steel safe, as tall as a man. Stine produced a key on a chain from his pocket, placed the key in a lock and turned it. Then he turned towards the stranger, in a daze, as if trying to understand what he was doing, and why this was happening. 'But I can't open it,' he said.

'Why not?'

'Because it requires two keys—and I have only one of them.'

'Where is the other?'

'Mr Crosby always kept it on his person. It must still be in his pocket.'

'Where have they taken Mr Crosby?'

'To the police station—for the police surgeon to conduct a post-mortem.'

At that moment the stranger reached out his hand, touched Robert Stine on the forehead, and issued a whispered command: 'Forget!' Immediately Stine collapsed in a heap on the floor.

He was found a few minutes later by his chief clerk.

'Mr Stine! Mr Stine! Are you all right? What happened?'

'I don't know,' muttered Stine, as he regained consciousness. 'I must have fainted.'

'What are you doing here, in the strongroom, sir? And why do you have you key out?'

Stine looked foolishly at the key in his hand, and murmured, 'I don't know—I really don't know.'

4

When Sherlock Holmes, Inspector Lestrade and myself emerged from our rooms into Baker Street, we found that the fog had closed in.

'It's becoming a real pea souper,' shivered Lestrade, as he turned up his coat collar.

I hailed a passing four-wheeler cab, and the three of us climbed on board.

'Where to, sir?' asked the driver.

'Bow Street police station,' said Lestrade. 'That's where we've taken the bodies of both victims of the vampire killer, Mr Holmes—that's what you said you wanted to see.'

'Quite correct, Lestrade. I wish to see for myself that the murder methods are identical.'

'Holmes,' I said, 'about this Doctor Defoe. How can you be so confident that he is behind these vampire murders?'

'Since the death of Professor Moriarty, Watson, there is no one in London—I venture to say, no one in the world—more likely to be behind a hideous new form of murder than Doctor Defoe. He delights in taking science to new depths of depravity. And he mixes the best of our western science, with strange occult sciences he has learned in the east.'

'Is that what he's done in this case?' I asked.

'It is a capital mistake, Watson, to theorise before you have all the evidence. It biases the judgement.'

'What about Mr Bunyan's suggestion of vampires—I mean real vampires. Could such creatures be more than just legend?'

'Rubbish, Watson, rubbish! What have we to do with walking corpses who can only be held in their grave by stakes driven through their hearts? It's lunacy. Are we to give consideration to such things? This agency stands flatfooted upon the ground and there it must remain. The world is big enough for us. No ghosts need apply.'

As our cab clattered through the fog, with the noises of London surging around us, I found it easy to believe that vampires were nothing but figments of a twisted imagination—believed in by none but village peasants in remote corners of Europe. But I also remembered how differently I had felt, standing in a dark alley over a body that had been drained of every drop of its blood.

Upon our arrival at Bow Street police station, Inspector Lestrade escorted us directly to the mortuary. In a cold, glum, cement-lined room were rows of tables. Two of these were occupied, and covered with green sheets.

'Here's this morning's victim,' said Lestrade, pulling down one sheet. 'And this one was found two days ago.'

'Look at them closely, Watson,' said Holmes. 'I'd value a medical man's opinion.'

'Certainly, old chap.'

Both victims appeared to be little more than skeletons draped in dry, parchment-like skin. Both were as dried and shrunken as an Egyptian mummy. I said as much to Holmes.

'It looks as though both have been subjected to some sort of instant mummification.'

'Yes, it does, doesn't it? And, of course, one of the first steps in mummification is the removal of all of the subject's blood.'

'Before post-mortem clotting sets in?'

'Precisely, Watson. Now, what's this on their hands,' continued Holmes, leaning more closely over the bodies. 'Lestrade, did your surgeon's report say anything about the hands?'

'The hands, Mr Holmes? I don't think so. Both reports were occupied by the baffling method of death. The hands didn't come into it.'

'Well, they should have done,' snapped Holmes firmly. 'Look closely—in both cases the skin on the hands is white and peeling: clear evidence of acid burns.'

'Acid burns?' muttered Lestrade. 'Well, there you are being fanciful, Mr Holmes. Why should these two murder victims have acid burns on their hands?'

'That, Lestrade, is an excellent question. And one

we must answer if we are to get to the bottom of this. Now, I'd like to take a look at the victims' clothing, if I may.'

'Yes, of course, Mr Holmes. I'll have the constable fetch it.'

A moment later a uniformed constable returned to the mortuary with an embarrassed expression on his face. 'I have the Chinese sailor's belongings here, Inspector,' he explained, 'but all of Mr Crosby's clothing and possessions were collected by the officer you sent, sir.'

'I sent? I sent no one!' snorted Lestrade.

'But he had an authorisation from you, sir, and so we handed over the things. Did we do the wrong thing, sir?'

'I smell the hand of Doctor Defoe in this,' said Holmes earnestly. 'Who else would have the daring to take what he wanted from a police station.'

'I do believe you're right, Mr Holmes,' said Lestrade. 'What can we do about it?'

'Do? Why nothing at all, Inspector. This time the evil doctor has been a step ahead of us. We must ensure that next time we are a step ahead of him.'

Holmes and I took our leave of Inspector Lestrade, who was still berating the poor young constable, and stepped out of the police station into a fog that reduced midday to a dim gloom.

'Cab, gentlemen?' called a voice from just a few feet ahead of us in the swirling fog.

'Climb aboard, Watson,' said Holmes. 'This is the cab we want.'

'If you say so, old chap. 221B Baker Street, cabbie,' I shouted as I stepped aboard, 'and make it lively.'

The cab set off at a cracking pace, and it was some little while before I realised that we were going in the wrong direction.

'Perhaps the fog has confused my sense of direction, or the cab driver's, but surely we're heading towards the docks, not Baker Street?' I said.

'Quite correct, Watson,' said Holmes. 'Exactly as I expected.'

'I don't understand?'

'When was the last time, Watson, that you were *offered* a cab in the middle of a London, pea soup fog?'

'Well . . . now you mention it . . .'

'Exactly. This cab picked us up because it had been sent for us.'

'But who sent it? Where are we being taken?'

'Surely you can guess, Watson. We are being taken to meet the most evil man in the world—the malevolent, ingenious Doctor Grimsby Defoe!'

5

'But surely Holmes we should escape, before this cab carries us all the way to Doctor Defoe's lair,' I protested.

'I should have warned you, old friend—I'm sorry about that,' said Holmes. 'But I am determined to meet the evil doctor—whatever the risk.'

'In that case—so am I,' I said.

'Good old, Watson,' said Holmes with delight. 'What would I do without you?'

I peered out of the cab, but could see nothing but dense, white, swirling fog. However, shortly the clatter of the horse's hooves on cobblestones changed to a harsher, flatter sound as dark shadows fell around us, and we came to halt.

'The cab has been driven into a building of some sort,' said Holmes.

Cautiously we both descended from the cab, and found ourselves standing in a deserted warehouse. The building was plunged into ominous shadows, and fingers of fog drifted through the air where the doors of the building had been closed behind us.

Just then a lantern appeared ahead of us, and a voice called, 'If you will step this way, please gentlemen.' We walked towards the voice, and the dim glow of light in that cavernous gloom. As we drew closer I could see a small group of men in that pool of yellow light. Several of them were large, heavily built, solid men with blank expressions. In the midst of them, seated in a high-backed chair on a raised platform was a man in a dark suit and a black cape. He had a lean and cat-like appearance, with a closely shaven skull, a small black beard, and the most remarkable green eyes.

'I am disappointed in you,' said Holmes calmly. 'So many guards around you—do you really fear me so much?'

'Fear you, Mr Holmes? Not in the least,' hissed the man I took to be the fiendish Doctor Defoe. 'My nerves are as strong as steel. My guards are here simply to ensure that you do nothing foolish, nothing that might end in your own injury—or death.'

Motionless I stood there, staring at the most dangerous man in the world. There was a menacing aura surrounding Dr Defoe, a feeling of the vast resources he commanded, a sense of the phantom army of criminals who would obey his every command.

'You have intruded upon my plans, Mr Sherlock Holmes,' said the evil doctor. 'There are others who will die from the fangs of my vampire killers before my plans are complete and I am ready to announce my demands to a terrified city. If you interfere with my operations, Mr Holmes, you will be among those who die.'

'Then you are not planning to kill us immediately?' asked Holmes coldly.

'If you thought that a possibility, you would not have allowed yourself to be brought here,' said Dr Defoe. 'You see, Mr Holmes, I do not underestimate your powers. I would advise you not to underestimate mine.'

'Then tell us why we are here, or let us go,' I demanded angrily. Holmes laid a restraining hand upon my arm. 'Steady, Watson,' he murmured quietly.

'My purpose in bringing you here,' continued the malevolent figure before us, 'is to invite you to join me. Imagine the irresistible power we could exercise if your great brain was joined with mine. The world would be at our feet, Mr Holmes—the entire world. Surely you of all people realise that the power of darkness is greater than the power of light. You are on the losing side, Mr Holmes, and I deplore the waste of your great intellect. Join with me, Holmes,' hissed the evil doctor, leaning forward eagerly, 'and help command my armies of the night.'

'Never!' snapped Holmes firmly. 'Kill me if you will, but for as long as you pursue your evil schemes I remain your implacable enemy.'

'A pity,' replied Grimsby Defoe, leaning back in his chair. His heavy eyelids half closed, reducing those magnetic green eyes to little more than slits. 'We could have done so much together. But never mind. I have too much respect for you to imagine that your answer is not final—I am quite sure that it is. As for killing you . . . well, yes, it may come to that, but for the time being a rather less drastic solution will apply.'

Defoe gave a small nod of his head, and Holmes and I were seized from behind by powerful hands. As we struggled to free ourselves our faces were covered with folded cloth. I caught a brief whiff of chloroform, and then fell into unconsciousness.

How long I was senseless I don't know. I awoke to find Holmes standing over me, an anxious expression on his face.

'How are you, old chap?' he asked.

'Still a bit woozy,' I replied, as I staggered to my feet. 'Where are we?'

'Still in the warehouse,' replied Holmes. 'But Doctor Defoe and his thugs have vanished.'

At that moment there was a low, booming roar—the sound of a boat on the river.

'I take it we're somewhere near the docks, then?' I asked.

'Correct. I have known for sometime that Defoe's headquarters were somewhere in or near Limehouse.'

'Is that what this building is, then—Dr Defoe's headquarters?'

'Certainly not, Watson. The man is far too cunning to meet with us in his own secret hideout.

No, this was simply a convenient, empty warehouse that he chose for his purpose. If you are fully recovered, old friend, it's time for us to leave. They have thoughtfully left the doors unlocked.'

'That was careless, surely?'

'It was arrogance, Watson, not carelessness. Defoe is so certain he is in control of the game that he believes we cannot touch him.'

'I see. Well, what can we do then?'

'Discover what foul plot he is hatching, and stop him, Watson—stop him before the whole of this great city has fallen into his claws.'

'The whole city?'

'Remember, Watson? He boasted that that was his goal. He talked about announcing his demands to "a terrified city". Whatever he is planning, it is worse than these vampire murders—far worse.'

As we walked back to Baker Street through the swirling fog and the fading light of dusk, I asked, 'How could Doctor Defoe terrify an entire city?'

'That man is every bit as ingenious as he is evil,' replied Holmes, quietly. 'I underestimated him once in the past, I shall never make that mistake again. If he says that he is preparing to threaten the entire city, then we must believe that he is.'

When we arrived back in our rooms there was a visitor waiting for us, a young woman—Mrs Catherine Crosby, looking pale and frightened.

'You shouldn't be out of bed, my dear,' I said, hurrying to her side. 'You are still not fully recovered from the shock of your husband's death.' I took her hand and led her to a comfortable chair.

'I did not intend to leave my bed, or my room,' said the young woman, as she ran a hand across her pale forehead. 'I just did. But I don't remember doing so. I became so frightened, that I came here at once. Oh, Mr Holmes—what is happening to me?'

'Tell me exactly what happened,' said Holmes, throwing his lanky frame into an armchair. 'Omit no details.'

'Well . . . I was lying in bed, in my room . . . resting. Just as Dr Watson had told me to,' she said. 'Mrs Newbigin, the housekeeper from the vicarage sat with me for a while. And then she left, as she had to prepare the vicar's supper. I must have dozed off. When I woke up I was no longer in my bed, I was standing in the alley behind the bank, and in my hand were two keys—these two keys.'

Holmes took the two small, silver keys from her, and examined them closely.

'Yale keys,' he said, 'of the type that would be used for a vault or a safe.'

'That's it!' cried Catherine Crosby. 'I thought they looked familiar. They are the keys to the main vault in the strong room of the bank. My husband always carried one in his fob pocket on the end of a chain. His chief accountant, Mr Stine, had the care of the other. But how did they come to be in my possession, Mr Holmes? And how can I have been moved from my bed to that horrible dark alley without my knowledge?'

'Tell me, Mrs Crosby, have you had any visitors in the last few hours?' asked Holmes. 'In particular were you visited by a tall, lean man with a closely shaved skull and a short black beard. You would have noticed his eyes in particular—long, magnetic eyes of the true cat green.'

28

'Why, Mr Holmes—this is remarkable! I have had no such visitor, but I have had the most vivid dream about just such a man.' She proceeded to tell us the whole story.

'That was no dream,' Holmes said grimly. 'That visitation was perfectly real.'

'But how could he have got past Mrs Newbigin?'

'There are few things that Dr Grimsby Defoe cannot do. During his visit he undoubtedly hypnotised you, and planted in your brain a posthypnotic command. It was in obedience to that command that you rose from your bed and went to the strong room of the bank.'

'But where did she get the keys from, Holmes?' I asked.

'Crosby's key was on a chain in his fob pocket. That key was taken from Bow Street police station by one of Dr Defoe's agents, by deception—remember, Watson?'

'Ah, yes, of course.'

'The other key has somehow been removed from Stine, the accountant. Both were then placed in the hands of this young lady here, while she was acting under the influence of Dr Defoe's evil hypnosis. I have no doubt that she used the keys to remove from the bank vault the "property" that Defoe was so desperate to recover.'

Catherine Crosby shuddered involuntarily. 'Oh,' she said, 'the thought of that man invading my mind, and having control of me . . .'

Just then the door of our rooms burst open and

Wiggins, the young street urchin rushed in.

'There's another . . .' he began shouting, but then recollected his manners and, taking off his filthy cap, said more quietly, 'Beggin' your pardon, Mr Holmes—but there's another dead 'un. Just like the first, 'e is. I thought you'd like to know.'

'Indeed I do. Well done Wiggins,' said Sherlock Holmes as he tossed the boy a sovereign. 'Can you show us where he is?'

'Yes sir, I can, Mr Holmes. It was one of my mates what found the cove.'

'Then we shall come with you at once. Mrs Crosby, you stay here for the time being. I'll send Mrs Hudson up to keep you company. Come along, Watson—grab your hat and coat. Murder calls us.'

Wiggins led us at a lively pace down Baker Street until he came to a halt in front of the vicarage where Henry Bunyan dwelt. The street urchin leaned over the iron railings that separated the house from the street, and pointed down the narrow flight of steps that led to the basement.

'Down there,' he said. Following his pointing finger, Holmes and I saw what looked like a bundle of clothing lying at the foot of those steps. Just then the Reverend Henry Bunyan stepped out of his front door.

'Mr Holmes, Dr Watson—have you come to visit me?' he asked.

'We come on a much more grisly purpose than that, I'm afraid,' Holmes responded. Turning to young Wiggins he added, 'Run and fetch a policeman for us.'

'Sure thing, Mr Holmes—I'll find you a copper.'

As the young lad sprinted down the street, Holmes, Mr Bunyan and myself gathered at the foot of the basement steps. Pulling back the loose clothing, Holmes revealed the dead man's face—a withered and shrunken face. The dried, parchment-like skin was pulled tightly over the skull. I conducted a rapid examination, and then reported, 'Identical to Crosby, the banker—this body has been drained of every last drop of blood.'

'Dr Defoe's infernal vampire killer has struck again,' Holmes muttered grimly.

'Vampire?' interrupted Mr Bunyan. 'So, you agree with me then—this looks like the work of a vampire?'

Holmes didn't respond, but searched the dead man's pockets. The dusk had turned into darkness, and we were working by the yellow glow of the nearest gas lamp, somewhat dimmed by the thick fog that still filled Baker Street.

'His name was Stine,' said Holmes, returning papers to the man's pockets.

'Crosby's accountant from the bank?' I asked.

'Precisely, Watson. And we know why he was killed—to obtain the second key to the vault. This poor wretch had the misfortune to cross the path of Dr Defoe—and he has suffered a horrible fate.'

31

7

An hour later we sat in the parlour of Mr Bunyan's house, as a mortuary van removed the shrunken, bloodless corpse from his basement steps. We had been joined by Inspector Lestrade from Scotland Yard. Our conversation was interrupted by a knock at the door.

'Come in,' said Henry Bunyan.

In response, his housekeeper, Mrs Newbigin, appeared in the doorway.

'There's a young lad here,' she said, with a sour expression on her face, 'a rather scruffy young lad— he says Mr Holmes wants to see him.'

'That will be Wiggins,' Holmes said. 'Send him in at once.'

When Wiggins entered the room he was not alone. Being dragged reluctantly along behind him was another filthy street urchin.

'This is my mate,' explained Wiggins. 'The one what you told me to fetch. The one what found the dead 'un.'

'Excellent,' said Holmes. 'And what is your name, young man?'

The second urchin stared at his boots in awkward silence.

'Simpkins is 'is name, Mr Holmes,' offered Wiggins, adding, 'Now you speak up for yourself,' as he dug his young friend sharply in the ribs.

'Tell me, Simpkins,' said Holmes gently, 'how did you come to find the body?'

'I went down to knock at the basement door,' replied the lad, 'lookin' for work. Mrs Newbigin sometimes pays me a shilling to wash the winders. But I never got to knock on the door—'coz I sees this body lyin' there.'

'Did you see anyone else around at the time—near this building, or anywhere in the street?'

'I'm afraid not, Mr Holmes,' Simpkins replied. 'I didn't see nuffin'. I'd tell you if I'd seen anyfink— honestly. But I could 'ardly see a thing—not with this fog.'

'So there was nobody about at all?' interrupted Inspector Lestrade. 'Now, I want you to be straight with me boy, I'm from Scotland Yard.'

'I am bein' straight,' protested the lad. 'There wasn't another 'uman bein' in sight.'

'There was nothing at all? No sign of any movement?' persisted Holmes.

'There was no people,' repeated the boy firmly. 'but I saw a snake. Or, I think I saw a snake. But that was the only living thing in sight.'

'A snake?' asked Holmes. 'Are you sure?'

'Not real sure,' Simpkins admitted. 'It sort of slithered out of sight into the storm drain as I was comin' down the steps. But it looked like a snake to me—an ugly serpent.'

'Describe it to me,' Holmes said, leaning forward, his eyes gleaming with interest.

'Well . . . it was . . . like a snake, you know. Slimy lookin' thing. It was a dark red colour, sorta like the colour of blood.'

'How large was it?'

'As thick as me arm.'

'And it vanished into the drain, you said?'

'Yeah. There's a drainage 'ole in the corner of the basement area. It disappeared down there.'

'You've done well, Simpkins. You too, Wiggins,' said Holmes, tossing each boy a shilling. As they left the room he turned to us and added, 'At last! A gleam of light in our darkness.'

While we were speaking, another event was happening, of which I learned only later. In fact, we were able to reconstruct the events only much later, based on the police reports.

At one of the main pumping stations for London's water supply, the shift was changing. Bert Hillyard arrived to begin his solitary night shift, carrying a packet of sandwiches and a bottle of beer. As the men of the day shift left, he locked the pumphouse door behind them.

He shovelled coal into the boiler of the big steam pump, looked at the pressure gauges, and then settled down at a bench to read the evening paper.

Bert quite liked the night shift. The hours were inconvenient, of course, and he had to work alone— but there was less work to do, and Bert was a touch on the lazy side.

An hour later he was still reading the paper when he thought he heard a noise. He put down the paper, cocked his head to one side and listened carefully. Nothing.

'I must have imagined it,' he told himself.

But a few minutes later he heard it again—quite clearly. It was a scratching sound, and it seemed to come from the far side of the pump house. Bert put down his paper, checked the pressure gauges on the main pump again, and walked slowly towards the far wall.

Before he was halfway across the floor, the noise came again—louder this time. Then it stopped, and the place was silent once more—except for the steady, wheezing thump of the brass engine.

Bert Hillyard put one ear against the wall and listened intently. The scratching was definitely there—and it was continuous. He realised then what was happening—something was constantly active on the other side of the wall, but he could only hear it over the sound of the engine on those rare occasions when it became louder.

He stood there puzzled, scratching his head. What could be making that sort of noise on the other side of a solid brick wall? A patient man, with plenty of time on his hands, Bert pulled out a wooden chair, and sat down—staring at the wall.

Twenty minutes later his patience was rewarded: he saw some dust falling out from the mortar around a row of bricks in the wall. And a moment later, one of the bricks began to move, as though it was being loosened from behind. Bert hurried back to his tool box and fetched a heavy spanner, then returned to the far wall. By now the bricks were being removed, one at a time, from the other side. In the steadily increasing hole Bert could see only blackness.

He crept towards the black, irregular hole that had appeared in the wall of the pumphouse, his large shifting spanner raised high and ready to attack. The sounds had now stopped entirely, the bricks were no longer being removed, and there was no sign of any movement of any sort.

Bert Hillyard stood looking at the black cavity in the wall. Then, when there was no sound and no movement, he crept a little closer. Being a naturally cautious man, it took him a full ten minutes to actually reach the hole in the wall. He could still see nothing but pitch blackness beyond. He put down his spanner, and lit a spare candle that was sitting on a work bench. Holding the flickering candle high, he thrust his head and shoulders into the black cavity.

He caught a glimpse of some movement.

It wasn't a human movement. It was more sinuous, and snakelike than that.

Then something came within the range of his flickering candle—something long, and slimy and blood-red. Terrified, Bert's scream was frozen on his lips. Recovering his wits, he turned to leave, but as he did so, the thing reared up like a cobra and struck.

Bert tried to fight it off with his hands, but it was too slippery, too slimy to get a grip on. The creature lunged at his neck, he felt a momentary burning sensation—and then he felt nothing.

Holmes and I took our leave of Inspector Lestrade at the doorway to 221B Baker Street. As we mounted the stairs Holmes suddenly stopped.

'Watson!' he cried, 'there's something wrong.'

'How can you tell, old chap?'

'Can't you smell it, Watson?'

I sniffed the air. 'By George, you're right—there is something. It's a faint whiff of . . .' I sniffed again, '. . . of . . . chloroform!'

'And that means Doctor Defoe. Hurry, Watson!'

So saying Holmes sprinted ahead of me up the stairs. By the time I reached the door of our sitting room, Holmes was lifting an unconscious Mrs Hudson onto the settee. There was no sign of Catherine Crosby.

'What's happened?' I gasped.

By way of reply, Holmes passed me a note that was lying on the table. It read, 'If you interfere with my plans, the young lady shall die.' The note was unsigned, but there could be no doubt who the message was from.

A low moan from the settee told us that our landlady was regaining consciousness. I lifted Mrs Hudson into a sitting position and waved a bottle of smelling salts under her nose.

'Where am I? What happened?' she murmured.

As I poured a glass of brandy for her, Holmes responded to her question with a question of his own. 'What can you remember, Mrs Hudson?'

'Well,' she said, sipping the brandy, 'I remember the policemen arriving.'

'Policemen?'

'Two uniformed constables. They said you had sent them, Mr Holmes—to keep an eye on Mrs Crosby until your return. I offered to make them a pot of tea. And then, when I turned my back on them I smelled this horrible smell, and then . . . well, that's all I can remember, I'm afraid.'

'That's quite enough,' said Sherlock Holmes grimly. 'His actions are bold, Watson—very bold. To send his men in police uniforms is a sign of his twisted genius.'

'What can we do, Holmes?'

'Think! I must think, Watson.'

'But Mrs Crosby—we must do something. She's little more than a girl, only nineteen years old. We can't leave her in the hands of that evil beast.'

'We can do so, Watson, for we must—we have no choice at this moment. You must understand, Watson, that Defoe will not harm her as long as she is useful to him. No—the best thing, the only thing, is to think. Think. Think!'

With these words Holmes threw off his jacket and reached for his violin case. As he removed the instrument from its case his eyes already had a distant, far away look. He tucked the violin under his chin, closed his eyes, and began to play. It was a haunting, sorrowful melody that swept and soared and filled the room.

Holmes was still playing when Mrs Hudson, now fully recovered, went to prepare supper. And he was playing still when she returned with a tray. I ate alone. I knew Holmes when these moods took him. He became unaware of food, of time, of everything except the soaring music, and the private world of deep concentration into which he had retreated.

He was still playing when I went to bed later that night. I woke up in the morning to silence. Pulling on my dressing gown I walked down to our sitting room. Holmes, his eyes red from lack of sleep, had laid aside the violin, and was pacing, restlessly, up and down.

'Morning, Holmes,' I yawned. 'Was it a fruitful night?'

'It was, Watson—I have a plan of action. Kindly summon Mrs Hudson for me, Watson. I want a big breakfast—bacon, kidneys, toast, coffee. I am famished. And over breakfast I will explain my plan to you.'

This, however, was not to be. Before I called for Mrs Hudson, our door burst open and Inspector

Lestrade rushed in, looking dishevelled and untidy.

'There's been another,' he gasped.

'Another?' I asked.

'Another vampire murder.' And with those words he slumped into an armchair.

'Clearly we get no breakfast today,' muttered Holmes, 'but we can at least have some coffee. Lestrade certainly looks as though he needs it.'

A few minutes later, Mrs Hudson arrived with a pot of steaming hot coffee, as Lestrade told us his news.

'It was the man on the night shift at the Battersea pumping station, Mr Holmes. His withered, shrunken body was found lying on the concrete floor, beside the main pump, early this morning when the first shift of the day arrived.'

Over coffee Lestrade gave us more details of the grim discovery. Then a brisk journey by cab took us to the scene of the latest horrible death.

'Who discovered the body?' asked Holmes, as we stood looking down at the twisted, shrunken, mummified corpse—mere skin, and bone, and withered flesh, all the blood having been sucked out.

'I did, sir,' said a young workman in overalls, twisting a cloth cap nervously in his hands as he replied.

'Has the body been moved at all?'

'No, sir. This is exactly where we found poor Bert.'

'Exactly here? Between the machinery and the rear wall of the pump house?'

'Yes, sir. And what none of the lads here can understand is how Bert's killer got in, sir.'

'Please explain yourself,' said Holmes.

'Well, sir. There's only one set of doors into this building—the main double doors over there. They're big, heavy wooden doors, and they're kept locked at night.'

'Were they locked last night?'

'Yes, sir. Jonah, the foreman, had to use his key to get in.'

Holmes pulled his magnifying lens out of his pocket and began examining the ground around the corpse. He worked outwards, in steadily widening circles, until, near the rear wall he announced, 'This is very interesting—very interesting, indeed.'

'What is it?' asked Inspector Lestrade, as we hurried to the spot where Holmes was crouched on the floor.

'Mortar, Inspector—loose mortar from between the bricks. There's only a small amount of it, but there are signs that a much larger amount has been swept up and removed.'

'What does it mean, Mr Holmes?' asked Lestrade, as he lifted his bowler hat and scratched his head.

'It means that we know how the vampire creature entered the building. What is still not clear is—why? Why would Dr Defoe want to kill the night watchman at the Battersea pumping house? And what is the connection between this man, a Chinese sailor and Crosby the banker? We know the motive for the death of Stine the accountant—it was to obtain his key. But why were the others killed? And what is the link between them?

Half an hour later Sherlock Holmes and I stood on the street outside the pump house. The fog swirled around us, even thicker than the day before.

'The key, Watson,' muttered Holmes grimly, as we walked back towards Baker Street, our coat collars turned up against the fog and the damp, 'the key is locating Dr Defoe's secret headquarters. Only there can we discover what diabolical plan he has to terrorise the great city of London. Only there will we discover how to end the murderous attacks of his vampire creature. And it is there he will be holding Catherine Crosby.'

'So, how do we do it, Holmes?' I asked.

'Ah, I have given much thought to the problem, and I have conceived of a plan. A dangerous plan, and I cannot ask you to accompany me on it—to do so would be to risk your life.'

'You don't have to ask me, Holmes—I insist. If you are going to face this terrible danger, then I must be there too.'

'Good old Watson,' said Holmes with a hearty laugh, 'the old reliable. Very well then, if you insist . . .'

'I do.'

'Then the plan involves persuading Doctor Defoe to arrange for us to be personally escorted to his secret headquarters.'

'Impossible! He is far too cunning to do any such thing.'

'And I am just cunning enough to persuade him to, Watson.'

As we rounded the corner into the upper part of Baker Street we almost collided with two boys—street urchins in grubby clothes.

'Here is good fortune, Watson,' cried Holmes. 'Here is Wiggins, and his friend Simpkins—the very people I was looking for.'

'Mornin' Mr Holmes,' responded Wiggins, sweeping his grubby cloth cap off his head in an exaggerated gesture of respect. 'What can I do for ya?'

'You can begin by rounding up a dozen or more of your associates. Two dozen would be even better. Can that be arranged?'

'I can do it quick as a whistle, Mr Holmes,' Wiggins said, with a cheerful grin. 'Big job on, then?'

'There certainly is. As soon as you have your "troops" assembled, you are to come to my rooms for your instructions. Clear?'

'Clear as a bell. I'll 'op to it straight away. I'll see

you later Mr Holmes.' With those words both Wiggins and Simpkins disappeared into the fog.

'Is this a good idea Holmes?' I asked as we mounted the front steps of number 221B. 'Using an army of street urchins?'

'They are the best army of all, Watson, for they are the invisible army.'

'Invisible?'

'Precisely. No one pays any attention to them. They can go anywhere, and do almost anything without arousing the least bit of notice. They can act without attracting the attentions of Dr Defoe's many agents. They alone can carry out my plans without attracting the evil doctor's scrutiny.'

As we walked up our stairs and entered our pleasant sitting room with its blazing fire I asked, 'Wouldn't it be better to call in Lestrade and arrange for the police to act on this plan of yours?'

'Dr Defoe would know about it in an instant. Do you imagine that he doesn't have his agents even within the police force itself? For I can tell you that he does. On top of which, to fill the streets of Limehouse with uniformed police officers would be to announce our presence, and our plans, with a brass band.'

'Yes, I see what you mean,' I replied, as I rang for tea.

After tea Holmes retired to his room, and returned half an hour later disguised as Lascar sailor—and looking like a thorough ruffian. Indeed, so good was the disguise that if I had not known it to be Holmes I would not have recognised him. He left, saying that he would be out for most of the afternoon.

With the damp air causing my old war wound to give me some pain, I settled down in front of the fire with a copy of *The Times*. I'm afraid I must have fallen asleep, because it was dark when I awoke.

It was a knock on the door that woke me.

'Come in,' I grunted, still half asleep.

Our visitor was young Wiggins. 'I've rounded up all the coves I could find, Dr Watson,' he reported. 'What next?'

'That's up to Mr Holmes,' I replied, 'and he is still out. I suggest you wait here for his return.'

'Sure thing, Dr Watson,' said Wiggins, as he took a seat in the one of the armchairs. And then he added with a cheeky grin, 'Any chance of a cup of tea and a bite of supper while I'm waiting?'

I rang for Mrs Hudson and ordered supper for the lad and myself. Just as we finished eating the door swung open and Holmes burst in, still disguised as an evil and ruffianly Lascar.

'The game's afoot, Watson,' he cried. 'I'm glad you're here Wiggins, I have your orders for you.'

While I carried the tea tray back downstairs to Mrs Hudson's kitchen, Holmes briefed Wiggins on what he and his troop of street urchins were to do. As he spoke, Holmes removed his make-up and disguise.

When I returned to our sitting room Wiggins had gone.

'They are my own private police force,' said Holmes, 'my "Baker Street Irregulars". They won't let us down, Watson—of that I'm perfectly sure.'

'So what do you and I do now, Holmes?'

'We wait.'

'Wait?'

'Yes, Watson, we wait for the arrival of Dr Defoe's messenger.'

'Oh . . . I see,' I replied, although, in truth, I didn't see at all. But I have learned over the years to trust Holmes implicitly in such matters. Holmes himself ate a hearty supper, and then lay down on the settee to catch up on the sleep he had lost overnight.

He was still sleeping several hours later when Mrs Hudson opened the door and announced, 'There's a gentleman to see Mr Holmes.'

A distinguished looking middle-aged man with gray hair and wearing an evening suit, entered the room.

'Are you Mr Sherlock Holmes?' he enquired.

'No, I'm Dr Watson. This is Mr Holmes,' I said, indicating the reclining figure on the settee.

Holmes' eyes flickered open, he propped himself up on one elbow and asked, 'How may I be of assistance to you?'

'My name is Lord Carruthers,' said our visitor, 'and I beg you to come with me at once, Mr Holmes. It is of the greatest urgency.'

'Pray tell me what has happened.'

'It's my wife, Mr Holmes—she has been kidnapped.'

'Surely that is a matter for the police?'

'The note from the kidnappers threatened to kill

my wife if I informed the authorities. Who else can I turn to, Mr Holmes?'

'Dr Watson and I will come with you at once,' replied Holmes, throwing off his lethargy as he pulled on his heavy Inverness cape and his deerstalker hat.

10

Minutes later Holmes and I were sitting in the back of Lord Carruthers's private coach as it clattered through the streets, the coachman constantly whipping the horses to greater and greater effort. Lord Carruthers sat opposite us, pale with concern and too anxious to converse.

The only remark that Holmes made was, 'This promises to be a most interesting evening, Watson'—and this he muttered quietly under his breath so that only I could hear.

I couldn't see where we were going, since curtains had been drawn over the windows of the coach, and with the silence around me, all I could hear was the rattle of the coach wheels on the cobbles.

'Is it much further?' I asked Lord Carruthers.

'Not far now,' his lordship replied, and lapsed once more into silence.

Shortly after this exchange, his lordship took a large, white handkerchief out of his top pocket and held it over his mouth and nose. This unusual gesture I assumed was to cover the grief, anxiety and distress he was feeling over the abduction of his wife. A moment later I became aware that a strange, green mist was drifting into the coach from a small pipe that seemed to be located just behind Holmes and myself.

'I say,' I began, 'have you noticed . . .'

'Indeed I have,' interrupted Holmes. 'I'll speak to you again at the end of our journey.' With that he inhaled deeply several times and promptly fell asleep! I also found myself becoming drowsy, and, after a moment's thought, I put this down to the green mist.

'Holmes!' I shouted, shaking his shoulder, 'we're being gassed.' I glanced across at Lord Carruthers, and found his eyes to be hard, cold, and cunning. I opened my mouth to protest, but before I could say another word sleep overwhelmed me.

As I slowly drifted back into consciousness I found myself to be in a long, low room. The heavy wooden beams supporting the ceiling not far over my head suggested that it might be a cellar. I was in a heavy, wooden chair, and, glancing to my right, I saw that Holmes was beside me. He was already awake and alert.

'Welcome back to the land of the living, Watson,' he said calmly.

'What's happened?' I began. Then as I tried to raise my hand to my head (which was aching badly) I discovered that I was tied to the chair with thick ropes. 'What's going on?'

51

'We have reached our goal, Watson,' said Holmes. 'We are in the secret headquarters of Doctor Defoe.'

'I don't understand. How do we come to be here?'

'My plan, Watson, you will remember was to have Defoe send his agents to fetch us—and my plan has worked.'

'How did you organise it?'

'In my disguise as a sailor and ruffian I haunted the pubs of Limehouse, and—I hope you don't mind, Watson—I made use of your name.'

'My name?'

'Yes, I spread the word the Dr Watson was boasting that his friend Sherlock Holmes had discovered the secret location of Doctor Defoe's lair. The rumour I started spread quickly, as I knew it would. Defoe's agents took it back to their master. It was a lure he could not resist. I knew he would find a way to draw us into his coils, and bring us to him.'

'And Lord Carruthers . . .?'

'A fraud. One of Defoe's agents.'

'So here we are.'

'Indeed, so here—as you so perceptively put it, old fellow—we are.'

'And much good it may do us!' I snorted. 'Really Holmes, this is most unwise. You have got us into the lair of the evil mastermind all right—but as *prisoners*!'

'Sshh Watson! I think I hear someone coming.'

The gaslights on the wall of the chamber had been turned up—clearly by some control outside the room—and I could now see our prison more clearly. It was a comfortably furnished cellar—a strange mixture of oriental luxury and scientific equipment. Down one long side was a bench filled with bottles of chemicals and laboratory glassware of all sorts. Tapestries and drapes covered the walls, and thick Persian rugs were spread over the floor. There were settees, cushions, and chairs of a Chinese design scattered about the room.

The sounds that Holmes' sharp ears had picked up now reached mine. There were soft noises coming from beyond an oak door at the far end of the room. The door swung slowly open, and in stepped Doctor Grimsby Defoe. Accompanying him were two large, and villainous looking, guards.

'We meet again, Mr Sherlock Holmes,' said Defoe as he walked towards us.

'The pleasure is all yours, I'm sure,' Holmes replied, seemingly unperturbed by the predicament we found ourselves in.

'Your nuisance value has now outweighed your entertainment value,' hissed the evil doctor in his strangely commanding voice, as he pulled his black cape more closely around his high shoulders. 'The time has come to solve my problem with Sherlock Holmes—and solve it permanently. But before I dispose of you, there are questions I want answered.'

Defoe snapped his fingers and one of his guards walked across to a wall tapestry and drew it to one side. Behind it, in a small alcove, was Catherine Crosby. She was tied to an upright wooden chair, and had a gag in her mouth.

'Young Mrs Crosby will die,' hissed Defoe with evil pleasure, 'if you refuse to answer. And she will die slowly, and painfully, I promise you.'

'You fiend!' I snapped, unable to contain myself any longer.

'Now, Mr Holmes,' said Defoe, completely ignoring me, 'will you cooperate?'

'It seems I have no choice.'

'A wise response. Now tell me this—how did you discover the location of my secret headquarters?'

'I will not lie to you Doctor Defoe,' said Holmes. 'The truth is, that I did not. I merely spread a rumour to that effect in order to arouse your interest.'

'For what purpose?'

'So that you would do as you have done—and bring me here.'

'You fool!' snarled Defoe. 'What good do you imagine it does you to be here—as my prisoner? And, I may add, a prisoner condemned to death, since I grow tired of your antics. What does this deception of yours accomplish?'

'It brings me face to face with you once again, Doctor, and gives me an opportunity to plead for the life of Mrs Crosby.'

'Do you imagine for one moment that I shall listen to your pleas?'

'I cannot believe that your heart is entirely black,' continued Holmes, unperturbed, 'and I appeal to whatever spark of your better nature is still left— however deeply it may be buried. This young woman plays no part in your plans. You have used her, now let her go.'

'Enough of this foolishness! All you have accomplished by this heroism, Mr Holmes, is her early death. She shall die beside you.'

11

Doctor Defoe clapped his hands, and poor Catherine
Crosby was dragged out of the alcove in which she
had been hidden. Her chair was then placed beside
ours. Her eyes were filled with tears and a look of
absolute terror.

'And now,' he said, 'I will leave you, Mr Sherlock
Holmes, and your companions to the horrible fate I
have planned for you.'

With these words the criminal mastermind turned
on his heels and walked out of the room. His guards
went with him, closing and locking the oak door as
they left.

As soon as we were alone Holmes began
struggling with the ropes that held him.

'It's no use,' I said, 'we're bound too tightly.'

'It's of every use, Watson,' said Holmes. 'In the
edge of this cape I have a blade—small but very
sharp. It's too small, and too well concealed, to be
discovered when our unconscious bodies were

searched for weapons—as I'm sure they were. Ah, yes, now I have it.'

As if by magic a small piece of glittering steel had appeared in Sherlock Holmes' right hand. Immediately he twisted around and began working the blade against the large knot that tied his wrists together.

Beads of sweat rolled down Holmes' face as he wrestled with that thick and solid knot. I began to fear that the small blade he was working with would prove inadequate for the task.

As he worked I heard, at the far end of the room, the faint sound of a panel sliding.

Holmes heard it too, for he stopped his struggle for a moment and asked, 'What was that?'

'I'm not sure,' I replied, 'but I'm certain I heard something.'

Holmes returned to his task with renewed vigour and determination. Less than a minute later he cried triumphantly, 'I've done it!' At a glance I saw that his hands were now free. Instantly Holmes began untying his feet, and a moment later he was free and standing up.

'If you don't mind, Watson,' he said, as he rubbed his sore wrists, 'I'll see to the lady first.'

'Yes, of course, old chap—proper thing to do.'

Holmes released Catherine Crosby's gag, and immediately she began to sob aloud. He then untied her wrists and freed her from the chair she was bound to.

'Oh, Mr Holmes, Dr Watson, you can't imagine

how pleased I am to see you. But you heard what Doctor Defoe said—is it true? Will we all die?'

'You mustn't lose heart, Mrs Crosby,' Holmes said firmly, as he loosed the last of my bonds.

At that moment I thought I saw a movement in the shadows on the far side of the room. It was only a small movement, and quite close to the floor.

'What is it, old chap?' asked Holmes, noticing the way I was staring.

'Perhaps it's nothing, Holmes—it's just that I thought I detected a movement of some sort.'

'In that case we must act quickly. See that ventilator up near the ceiling?'

'Yes, I see it, Holmes.'

'That will be at street level. We must get it open as quickly as we can. I will start work on it at once. You take a look at Mrs Crosby.'

'Very well, Holmes, but without my doctor's bag there's not very much I can do.'

I checked Mrs Crosby's pulse rate, rubbed her sore wrists, and asked her how she felt.

'I'm all right,' she responded quietly. In truth, she was a healthy young woman, and the only damage had been to her nerves—but that had been considerable.

Holmes had climbed onto the table containing the bottles of chemicals, and was undoing the screws that held the ventilator panel in place. Suddenly, Catherine Crosby screamed loudly in my ear.

'What is it?' called Holmes, as he spun around.

'There's . . . something . . . something moving

under that table . . . in the shadows,' she gasped.

'Watson—keep your eyes open,' snapped Holmes as he resumed his task. I stared at the place indicated to me by the frightened young lady at my side. The shadows in the room were deepest under the table, despite which I too thought I could detect movement there.

'Got it!' said Holmes triumphantly as he removed the ventilator and revealed a small, oblong opening onto the street at pavement level. Holmes whistled loudly and a small, grubby face appeared at the opening. It was Wiggins!

'You had no difficulty following us then?' Holmes asked.

'Not through the streets of London, Mr Holmes—that's our 'ome, the streets of London.'

'Good lad. Now, send one of your most trusted boys to summon the police, and hand me down my equipment.'

'Righto, Mr Holmes.'

A moment later a small parcel wrapped in a piece of cloth was handed through the opening.

'Thank you, Wiggins. Now what I need is a diversion. Something noisy. A small riot would do.'

'We can manage that, Mr Holmes. In a few minutes from now there'll be so much noise that no one in the building overhead will be able to 'ear themselves think—let alone 'ear anythink you're doing.'

With these words the face of Wiggins vanished as he went off to organise a "riot" with his gang of street urchins. Holmes stepped from the table onto the floor and began unwrapping the parcel.

'What is it, Mr Holmes?' asked Catherine.

'A small bottle of nitroglycerine, Mrs Crosby.' In response to her expression of alarm he added, 'Only a very small bottle, I assure you—just a few drops are needed to blow that heavy oak door off its hinges.'

I must admit that I shared Mrs Crosby's concern. As a medical man I knew enough chemistry to know just how unstable the clear, oily liquid known as nitroglycerine can be.

As Holmes hurried up to the door and began making his preparations Mrs Crosby spoke again. 'There!' she said, 'I saw it again—in the shadows underneath that long table. There is definitely something moving there.'

Holmes was concentrating too intently to pay much attention to her remark. He set two small drops of nitroglycerine on each of the door hinges, with a long fuse connecting them.

'There, that's done,' he announced as he turned back towards us, and handed me the bottle of nitroglycerine for safe keeping. At that moment, a dark, sinuous shape shot out of the shadows under the table right at his feet.

'Holmes!' I cried out in warning. 'Look out!'

But even as I spoke the creature seemed to rear up like a cobra, and then strike forward in a powerful blow, attaching itself to Holmes' throat.

12

Holmes staggered backwards, clutching at the creature that had attached itself to his throat. I rushed to his assistance. The creature was as thick as a man's arm, and snakelike in appearance. But when I tried to grapple with it, I found it to have the slippery, slimy feeling of a large slug. It appeared to have no scales, but to be covered by a tough, flexible hide that, in turn, was covered with a thick, greasy slime.

Where it had attached itself to Holmes' neck there appeared to be not a normal snake's head, but a flat, disc-like protuberance which, as I pulled against it, felt as though it was glued tightly to his skin.

The grip the creature had upon Holmes was so strong that we could not break it, even with both of us struggling against it. I reached out to the nearby table, picked up the heaviest glass jar I could find, and smashed it against the beast.

'Again, Watson. Do it again,' grunted Holmes, 'I can feel it weakening.'

I struck the creature again and again. At the fourth blow the jar shattered, the broken glass piercing the serpent's body and sending a great wave of blood over the floor. At this it lost its grip on Holmes, who staggered back against the wall, clearly exhausted.

The thing on the floor was still alive, thrashing about, and trying to rear up again. I grabbed another chemical container and threw it as hard as I could. It smashed and its chemical contents covered the creature causing some sort of reaction. There was a hiss of steam, a pungent odour, and the creature lay dead.

I hurried to Holmes' side. Blood was pouring out of a wound on the side of his neck. The wound had opened up a major artery, and the serpent's bite must have injected an anti-clotting agent, for Holmes was losing blood at a dangerous rate. He appeared to be unconscious.

As I tore strips from my shirt to make a bandage his eyes flickered open.

'Watson,' he gasped in a faint voice, every word a painful struggle.

'Don't talk, old chap, I'll soon have you patched up,' I said, with a confidence I did not feel.

'Watson,' whispered Holmes, more urgently. 'Do you have matches?'

'Matches? Why yes, I believe I have some in my pocket. But that hardly matters now . . .'

'Light the fuse, Watson. Blow the door. We must escape.'

Of course! He was right. The creature was only

part of our problem. We also had to escape from Doctor Defoe's evil clutches. By this time Catherine Crosby had reached my side. I completed the bandage and then the two of us dragged Holmes to the far end of the room. Mrs Crosby knelt beside Holmes, keeping the bandage firm against his still bleeding wound. I ran to the door, and with trembling fingers lit a match, and set it to the fuse. Then I ran back and joined the others.

There was a long, tense pause, and then a heavy, sharp explosion. As the smoke cleared I could see that the door was hanging off its hinges, and our way of escape was now clear. Hastily I picked up Holmes' small, dangerous bottle of nitroglycerine, wrapped it in cloth and stuffed into my pocket.

The sound of the explosion had been lost in the noise from the street, which, until that moment, I had not noticed. The sounds of shouting, and rioting echoed loudly from above. Wiggins had done his job!

Sherlock Holmes had lost consciousness, and it was with some difficulty that, with the assistance of Mrs Crosby, I carried him through the doorway, up a flight of stairs, through several deserted rooms, and out onto the street.

Wiggins was waiting for us.

'Cor! What's wrong with Mr Holmes?'

'He's been badly injured, Wiggins. Can you find me a cab? We must get him back to our rooms urgently.'

'Sure thing, Dr Watson. I'll 'ave a cab 'ere in a jiffy.'

Wiggins was as good as his word, and in less time than I could have imagined Holmes was being whisked away from the scene of his fearful encounter with the vampire creature. Mrs Crosby and myself continued our nursing of him during that cab journey.

Back in our rooms I cleaned the wound, applied antiseptic and a proper bandage. Then, with Mrs Hudson's help, I cleaned him up and put him to bed.

He was still unconscious, and his breathing was shallow and laboured.

'How is he?' asked Mrs Hudson anxiously. 'Will he be all right?'

'He's lost a great deal of blood, and, quite frankly, I don't know what will happen.'

'What can I do to help?'

'For the time being he has to rest. When he wakes he must be fed iron rich foods that will build up his blood.'

'I'll make him lots of beef tea,' said our kindly landlady, tears in her eyes.

'And the other thing you can do, Mrs Hudson, is to pray for his recovery.'

'Oh, I'll certainly be doing that, Dr Watson.'

I walked out of Holmes' bedroom, and into our sitting room to discover that Catherine Crosby was still there, and that she had been joined by the Reverend Henry Bunyan.

'How is Mr Holmes?' asked the vicar anxiously.

'In a dangerous condition,' I replied glumly. 'It will be days before we can know for sure whether he will survive or not. I would value your prayers.'

'I shall be praying most earnestly for his recovery.'

'Now then, my dear,' I said, turning to Mrs Crosby, 'how are you feeling?'

'Much recovered, thank you Dr Watson. Seeing what you and Mr Holmes were prepared to risk to rescue me from the clutches of that . . . that . . . fiend . . . well, it makes me forget all that I have been through.'

'I'm pleased to hear it,' I said wearily, as I sank into a chair.

'Mr Bunyan has very kindly suggested that I move in to the guest room in the vicarage for a few days—until I've fully recovered.'

'An excellent suggestion.'

'And during the day I will come down here and sit with Mr Holmes,' she continued. 'And help with the nursing of him back to health.'

'That's very kind of you.'

'It's the least I can do.'

Later, when they had left, I walked over to my old friend's bedside and looked down upon his unconscious form. When I saw the beads of sweat upon his pale skin, and the blood that was still soaking through his thick bandage, and when I heard his struggle to breathe—I was very much afraid that I was looking at a dying man.

13

The next two days passed in a kind of blur. I spent much of it wondering what kind of creature it had been that had attacked Holmes. It had left acid burns on his hands and on mine, so clearly the slime on its skin was acidic. But that got me no closer to identifying what it could be.

Time and again over those two days I would stand at the door of Holmes' room looking at the sleeping figure, and listening to his feeble breathing. Mrs Hudson and young Mrs Crosby took turns at sitting by his side.

I constantly checked his pulse and temperature and looked for any sign of improvement. I consulted with medical colleagues, and arranged for a specialist friend to visit and examine Holmes. Everything possible was done for him. But still he showed no signs of recovery.

After 48 hours I could stand it no longer. As a doctor I felt helpless. What else could I do? I decided to resume the investigation, to do what Sherlock Holmes would have done if he was fit and well. Where to begin? Well, the best place, I decided, was with the question that Holmes had posed, 'What links the murders of Crosby the banker, a Chinese sailor and a night watchman at a pumping station?'

In order to find out, I put on my hat and coat, and walked down Baker Street, through thick, swirling fog, to the Cox and Co. branch bank that Crosby had managed until his death. There I found the chief clerk, Frank Wells, and asked him to give me a few minutes of his time.

'Do you and Mr Holmes have any idea yet who killed poor Mr Crosby?' he asked.

'Not yet,' I admitted. 'At least, we believe that a certain criminal mastermind was behind what happened—what we don't know is exactly how or why. That's why I'm here—if you can tell me a little more about Mr Crosby himself that may help us.'

'I'll certainly do all I can, Dr Watson.'

'Fine. What sort of a man was he? How well did you know him?'

'Not very well, I'm afraid. I worked for him— that's all. I know he came from a modest family background and had earned his position as manager by his own hard work.'

'He married rather late, I take it?'

'Yes he married only six months ago—a woman some 20 years younger than himself. But they seemed very happy together.'

'Did he have any interests outside the bank?'

'None that I can think of . . . except for his being a bit of an amateur scientist, of course.'

'Amateur scientist?'

'That's right, Dr Watson. He used to go to public lectures on scientific subjects whenever he had the time. And he had quite a collection of books, he told me once, on chemistry and zoology, and all kinds of things that are a complete mystery to me, I'm afraid.'

'I see,' I muttered thoughtfully, trying to work out where this information got us. 'Thank you for your time, Mr Wells.'

As I walked slowly back to the rooms I shared with Holmes I pondered on the information I had received. There seemed to be so little in it, and yet, Holmes, I was sure, would see some significance there. He would analyse and form deductions from the facts I had collected. I seemed to hear his voice in my head, saying, as he had said so often, 'You know my methods, Watson.'

Yes, I had seen him at work on so many cases. I had recorded those cases in my notes. And yet, left to my own devices, I felt helpless, and quite unable to see the clear picture that Holmes would have grasped instantly.

I was still thinking these thoughts as I stood looking down once again at my friend's unconscious body. His face was very pale, and large drops of sweat stood out on his forehead. Mrs Crosby sat beside his bed, wiping his face with a damp cloth.

Seeing Holmes so helpless, and feeling so helpless

myself, I felt a sudden surge of determination. The investigation must continue—it must not be abandoned.

I went to my room, took my old army revolver out of a desk drawer, and loaded it with cartridges. Slipping it into my coat pocket, and putting on my hat, I returned to the street, and began walking towards Limehouse.

I remembered the building in which Holmes, Catherine Crosby, and myself, had been held prisoners—the building that was the den of Doctor Grimsby Defoe. As we had staggered onto the street I had noticed the building had a sign reading: 'Ballard and Phillips, Wine and Spirit Merchants, Offices and Warehouse.' If I could find that sign again, I could find Doctor Defoe.

What made my search difficult was the fog. It made the streets of Limehouse damp and depressing. And the thick fog was turned a dull brownish gray by smoke from coal fires. Mid-afternoon was like sunset on an overcast day. Amid this gloom I had to be close to each building to read the signs painted over the doorways.

My passion had become a quiet determination to find the evil doctor, and to stop him before more people died from his fiendish vampire creatures, and before he could complete his plans to terrorise the whole city of London.

As these thoughts were running through my mind, I looked up and saw a sign that read: 'Ballard and Phillips, Wine and Spirit Merchants, Offices and

Warehouse.' I had found it—the lair of Doctor Defoe!

I pushed open the office door and walked inside. It looked like a genuine office. I faced a wooden counter, behind which clerks worked at their desks.

'May I be of assistance to you, sir?' asked a surly man behind the counter.

'Yes, you may,' I replied. 'Please inform Doctor Defoe that Dr John Watson wishes to see him.'

'I'm afraid there's no one here of that name, sir.'

'My good man, I will not go away—I insist upon seeing Doctor Defoe.'

'Perhaps if you would care to take a seat in our waiting room, I will go and ask the office manager if he has heard of the man you are looking for.'

'Yes, thank you.'

He led me through a wooden door with a panel of frosted glass. Inside was a plain table, with several leather chairs.

'Please take a seat, Doctor . . .?'

'Dr Watson.'

'. . . while I make some enquiries.'

I took a seat and the sullen faced man left, being careful to close the door as he did so. I waited for ten minutes, and then for fifteen. When my watch showed that twenty minutes had elapsed I went to the door and turned the handle. That's when I discovered that I was locked in!

14

I rattled the doorknob and pounded on the frosted glass, but there was no response.

'Let me out!' I shouted. 'This is outrageous.'

From beyond the door there was nothing but silence. Taking my revolver out of my pocket, I turned it around, butt first, and smashed the glass panel. Then I reached through the shattered opening and unfastened the lock.

The office beyond was now completely deserted. The blinds had been drawn over the front windows of the office, and I found myself in a dim, gloomy twilight. I settled my revolver comfortably in my right hand, and began exploring the building.

Behind the front office was a maze of corridors—some opening into other, smaller, offices, others ending in locked doors or staircases. The whole building seemed to be empty. In none of my wanderings did I encounter a single living soul. Had Doctor Defoe left his lair? Had he relocated to another secret location?

At last my explorations brought me to a spot I vaguely recognised. It was staircase leading downwards, towards the cellars, and I had a suspicion that Catherine Crosby, Holmes, and myself had fled up those very stairs only two days earlier.

Taking a firmer grip on my revolver, I proceeded slowly downwards. My footsteps seemed to echo through that empty building. The lower I proceeded, the darker it became, until, at the foot of the stairs, I could see only by the very dimmest light reflecting down from the twilight above.

The stairs ended at a small landing, with three doors opening off the landing. I tried each door in succession. Two of them were locked. The doorknob on the third turned under my hand, and slowly I pushed the door inwards. It opened on a study— bookshelves lined the walls, thick carpet was on the floor, and an open fire cast a sinister red glow over the whole room. In the centre of the room was a large, mahogany desk, and, seated behind the desk, in a high backed chair, was Doctor Defoe himself.

'Come in, Dr Watson,' he said. 'I've been expecting you.'

'But you haven't been expecting this,' I said grimly, raising my revolver. Instantly I heard a door behind me open, and, before I could move, two huge hands, like steel vices, pinned my arms to my side.

'Disarm him!' snapped doctor. One of the large hands squeezed my wrist until the pain caused me to cry out, and drop the revolver. It was picked up by another of Doctor Defoe's servants who, I discovered, was silently hovering behind me.

'Now you may come in, Dr Watson,' said Defoe in his strangely powerful and commanding voice. 'Please take a seat.'

Strong hands on my shoulders propelled me forward, and pushed me into a leather chair facing the desk.

'Now tell me, Dr Watson, what brings you to see me?' asked the evil doctor.

'A determination,' I muttered, 'to complete what Holmes had begun.'

'Then Sherlock Holmes has already died?'

'He was still breathing when I left him.'

'What a pity. Still, he shouldn't last much longer.'

'I fear not.'

'And with Holmes out of the way—there is no one in London who can stop me.'

'I almost stopped you!'

'You didn't even come close, Dr Watson. You were watched, and I was kept informed of your progress, from the moment you entered the Limehouse district.'

'And the rest of it? Being locked up?'

'Just my little game, I'm afraid. I do like to amuse myself.'

For a long moment, the two of us stared at each other. I don't know what he saw in me, but I found a strange, evil fascination in the man I was looking at: the tall, lean, cat-like figure, the close-shaven skull, the short black beard, and those eyes—strange, compelling eyes of the true cat green. He was indeed as Holmes had described him—a brow like Shakespeare and a face like Satan.

'Would you like to know the truth about my plans, Dr Watson?' he hissed, in a voice that was little more than a whisper. 'Before you die, that is?'

'Yes,' I growled, 'yes, I would like to know what fiendish evil you have planned.'

'Good. Excellent. I would quite like to explain my plans to a medical man—such as yourself, Dr Watson. You will understand the full power of what I have in mind. Tie his hands behind his back, and then bring him.'

Instantly those same powerful hands grabbed my wrists and bound them so tightly as to be quite painful.

Doctor Defoe led the way down a short corridor, through a heavy oak door, and into the same long cellar in which Holmes, Mrs Crosby and myself had been held prisoners.

'Does this room bring back fond memories for you doctor?' asked Defoe. 'I hope it does. Take a seat there, on that settee, while I show you something.'

He walked over to the long bench with its bottles of chemicals and laboratory glassware. After pulling on a pair of thick rubber gloves, he lifted up a small, glass tube.

'Imagine, Dr Watson, if I was able to blackmail the government of this great nation. Imagine if I could demand a ransom payment of, let's say, one million pounds.'

'What sort of threat could you make that would be worth so much?'

'Let's say that I could threaten to kill a large proportion of the population of London. Would that be worth a million pounds?'

'It would be an empty threat. You could never carry it out. You would need thousands of those horrid vampire creatures of yours—whatever they are.'

'Oh, you needn't bother your head about my vampire killers—you shall meet one, very shortly.'

'I still say your threat against London would be a hollow one.'

'On the contrary, Dr Watson—this small glass tube I hold in my hand would make it very real. This tube contains the cholera bacterium.'

'You swine!'

'You see. I knew that a medical man would immediately see the reality of my threat. Cholera—a violently infectious disease from the orient, Dr Watson. Imagine it spreading through this densely populated city. Can you imagine that?'

'Have you no scruples?' I cried in despair.

'None at all, I assure you,' replied Defoe with a savage laugh.

15

Doctor Defoe held the glass tube in his hand thoughtfully.

'Yes,' he hissed maliciously, 'in here is the pestilence imprisoned. Only break such a little tube as this into a supply of drinking water. Say to these minute particles that one can only see under a microscope, and that one cannot taste or smell—say to them, "Go forth, increase and multiply" and death—mysterious, untraceable death, death swift and terrible, death full of pain and indignity—would be released upon this city, and go hither and thither seeking his victims. Have you nothing to say, Dr Watson?'

I could have said much, but it would have done no good. I held my tongue.

'My little agent of death, my little *Vibrio cholerae*, would be transmitted rapidly from place to place, from person to person. In one place it would take the husband from the wife, in another the child from its mother, in yet another the statesman from his duties and the workman from his work. My little agent of death would follow the water mains, creeping along streets, picking out and punishing a house here and a house there where they did not boil their drinking water, creeping into the vats of the cordial makers, getting washed into salad, and lying in wait in blocks of ice. He would soak into the soil and reappear in springs and wells at a thousand unexpected places—many of them far from London. Once start him in the water supply, and before the authorities can control him or stop him he will have slaughtered at least one tenth of the population of this great city.'

'This is demonic!' I cried. 'It must be stopped.'

'And it will be stopped—if the government pays me one million pounds. But I'm afraid I really cannot stay and talk to you much longer, Dr Watson. I am shifting my headquarters—you and Sherlock Holmes have made that necessary. Most of my staff have already left. So now I must draw this delightful meeting to a close, and join my staff at my new, secret, unfindable, headquarters. Farewell, Dr Watson.'

As he stood up he drew his black cloak more closely around his high shoulders.

'Oh, by the way,' he continued, 'you expressed some curiosity about my vampire killers. Well, you are about to meet one—at very close quarters. Tie his ankles and lay him on the floor.'

A moment after this order had been given my feet

were bound just as tightly, and just as painfully, as my wrists, and a gag was placed in my mouth. The last of Doctor Defoe's servants to leave the room placed a woven cane basket on the floor and removed the lid. Then he too left.

I lay there in the dim light that filtered through the repaired ventilator, wondering what would happen next. For a very long time, nothing seemed to happen, and the cellar was as silent as the tomb.

Then there appeared to be some movement in the basket. A dark, sinuous shape slithered over the top rim of the basket and began to slowly lower itself onto the floor. There was little I could see in that dark cellar, but I had no doubt it was identical to the vampire creature that had attacked Holmes, and that had proved so hard to kill.

Just what was it? I asked myself. Was it the origin of all the vampire legends? Was it some strange creature from the remote Carpathian Mountains—the supposed home of Count Dracula? Was it more than mere flesh and blood? Could it be some evil creature, some wicked power, that Doctor Defoe had lured into our world from another, more demonic, dimension?

At least I wouldn't have to wait to find out. Before long it was sure to become aware of my presence, and would attack me—leaving behind a shrivelled, shrunken, withered corpse, just like the others. As a Christian I was not afraid of being dead—of being ushered into eternity and into the presence of the living God—but the process of dying was another matter entirely. I didn't fancy the idea of passing from this world under the fangs of that . . . creature.

The thing slithered all the way out of the basket and onto the floor. Then it was still for a long time before it began moving in a strange, slug-like way across the carpet. It began, not by moving towards me, but towards the long bench. For some time I lost sight of it in the deeper shadows under the bench.

Then the thing emerged again. Its movements were slow and sluggish—as if it had not yet picked up the scent of a possible victim. I struggled as hard as I could against the ropes that bound my hands and feet. It was no good—I was tied up both expertly, and very tightly.

Unfortunately, my struggles attracted the attention of the thing—and it began to move slowly towards me. I tried to inch away, but my movements were too restricted. I was helpless. Like a sacrificial victim I could do nothing but lie there, waiting for death to come.

And come it did—slithering slowly and relentlessly across the floor.

Soon I became aware of a stale, swamp-like odour that was coming from the thing. And then it was less than an arm's length away. There was a long moment, as it seemed to be preparing itself, and then it raised up its forepart, like a cobra about to strike. I closed my eyes.

'This is it,' I thought, as I commended my soul to God's mercy. Just then, as I lay there with my eyes closed, waiting for the painful attack at any second, there was a loud crash, and I smelled smoke. I opened my eyes—and there was the thing, lying quite still in a pool of blood. I twisted around towards the doorway. There stood Sherlock Holmes, with a .45 calibre Webley revolver in his hand, with blue smoke drifting out of the barrel.

16

'Holmes! How on earth . . .?' I spluttered, as soon as he removed my gag.

'How are you, old fellow? Have you been hurt at all?'

'No . . . no . . . I am completely uninjured. But, you Holmes . . . I thought you were . . .'

'Dying?'

'Well, yes.'

'You have known me for a long time, Watson—you, of all people, should have known that my powers of recovery are remarkable. Basically I slept for two and half days, woke up, ate a hearty meal, and felt tired and sore, but well.'

'Holmes, you truly are remarkable. But how did you find me?'

'Once I had recovered, naturally, I asked for you. No one seemed to know where you had gone—neither Mrs Hudson, nor Mrs Crosby. An examination of your room showed that you had taken your old army revolver. That meant you were tackling something dangerous. I deduced an attack on Doctor Defoe. So, I armed myself and hurried here.'

'You have missed the evil doctor,' I explained, rubbing my sore wrists and ankles.

'Yes. Clearly he has fled from this lair. But he will have had another place prepared in advance.'

'He told me as much,' I said as I staggered to my feet. 'What about this . . . this thing, this creature?'

'We'll take the remains with us, Watson—perhaps in the basket that was used to transport it. A careful analysis and examination will tell us more.'

'Holmes!' I exclaimed suddenly. 'Doctor Defoe revealed his plans to me. He explained how he intends to terrorise this entire city.'

In as few words as possible I outlined Defoe's evil scheme for threatening to create a cholera epidemic unless the government paid him one million pounds.

'There is no end to the depths of that man's evil genius,' responded Holmes, when I had finished my tale. 'The road before us is a dark and difficult one, Watson. With all his resources and all his scientific powers, we must still find a way to stop him before many thousands of people die. Come on, old chap, back to our rooms to plan and prepare.'

And so it was that Holmes and I made our way back to Baker Street with our grisly souvenir—the carcass of the vampire creature.

Later that night Sherlock Holmes stood at his familiar work bench that was covered with old chemical stains—the place where he conducted all his experiments. Dressed in a rubber apron, and wearing strong rubber gloves, he cut slices out of the remains of the vampire thing. These he examined under his microscope, and tested with various chemical reactions.

At a late hour he finished his work, cleaned away the mess, and washed down the work bench with carbolic.

As he lit a pipe, to drown the smell of the carbolic soap, I asked him, 'Do you now know what sort of creature that was, Holmes?'

'Indeed I do, Watson. It is a freakish member of the genus *Haemadipsa*.'

'I'm just a plain medical man, Holmes—you'll have to explain.'

'It's a member of the leech family, Watson. I suspect that this freak has been specially bred from the giant red leech of Burma.'

'Specially bred?'

'Bred for extraordinary size and viciousness in attack. It was described as being a snake, or "snakelike", but strictly speaking it is a worm. You saw that instead of a head, it has a disc-like sucker. In the middle of the sucker is a mouth, surrounded with hundreds of small, razor sharp teeth. Its normal form of attack is to attach itself to its victim with this front sucker, make a wound, and then suck out blood. All bloodsucking leeches produce a liquid containing a chemical substance called *hirudin*. This prevents the blood from thickening and makes it easier for the leech to suck the blood.'

'Your description quite chills my blood, Holmes. But how did he do it? How did Doctor Defoe produce a leech of this prodigious size?'

'Be in no doubt, Watson, as to Defoe's genius. He is not only evil, he is brilliantly evil—and his scientific knowledge is profound. What sort of breeding or feeding program he has conducted to produce these monsters I cannot imagine. But I have no difficulty accepting that he has been able to do it.'

'Nor have I, Holmes—I've seen the hideous things!'

At that point our conversation was interrupted by a sharp knocking at our front door.

'Mrs Hudson will have retired for the night,' said Holmes. 'You had better admit our late night caller, Watson.'

'Certainly, Holmes.'

When I got downstairs and opened the front door, I found Inspector Lestrade standing on the doorstep.

'You'd better come inside, Inspector. It's freezing out there. And I think it's just starting to rain. What brings you here at this hour of the night?'

'An urgent message for Mr Holmes,' explained Lestrade. 'Which I was ordered to carry personally.'

On reaching our sitting room, Lestrade went straight to the fire to warm himself, as Holmes asked the same question I had, 'Why are you calling so late, Lestrade?'

'To bring you this, Mr Holmes,' replied the police officer, handing over a note.

Holmes read the note, and then handed it over to me.

'Why Holmes!,' I said after the first glance, 'this is from . . .'

'Yes, from Lord Salisbury.'

'. . . the Prime Minister. He wants a private meeting with you, at Number Ten Downing Street. Tonight. Immediately.'

'If you're ready, Mr Holmes,' said Lestrade. 'As much as I would rather stay by the fire, this is a matter of the utmost urgency.'

'In that case, we mustn't keep the Prime Minister waiting. Come along, Watson, grab your hat and coat, the weather is beastly outside.'

I pulled on a great coat, and soft felt hat. Sherlock Holmes wrapped his Inverness cape around his lanky form, and pulled his deerstalker cap on his head. We then hurried downstairs, leaped into the police coach that Inspector Lestrade had brought with him, and sped off into the night.

17

As our carriage rattled through the cold night streets, back in the vicarage of St Bede's on Baker Street there were events happening of which I learned only later.

The Reverend Henry Bunyan sat in his study, in the warm, yellow glow of a reading lamp, his head bent over a book. There was a quiet tap and then his study door swung open. It was young Mrs Catherine Crosby, and she was carrying a tray upon which sat a tea pot and a set of cups and saucers.

'My dear, you should be in bed,' exclaimed the clergyman.

'I couldn't sleep, Mr Bunyan,' she replied. 'So much has happened to me, and so much is on my mind that I simply couldn't sleep at all.'

'I quite understand my dear.'

'And I knew that you were in here studying, so I thought you might like a fresh pot of tea?'

'That's most thoughtful of you, and it's exactly what I feel like. Will you join me?'

The young woman sat down on the opposite side

of the large, oak desk and poured out two cups of tea.

'Is your room satisfactory?' asked Bunyan. 'I'm afraid the guest room is seldom occupied and, as a result, can be a trifle dusty.'

'It's very comfortable, thank you. And it's right next door to Mrs Newbigin's, which is very comforting. She said that she is a light sleeper, and that if she hears me crying out from nightmares she will come in and sit with me.'

'My housekeeper really is an excellent woman,' beamed the clergyman. Turning over the pages of the old book on his desk he continued, 'I have just been looking up some of the folklore pertaining to vampires, and I am forced to admit that it doesn't seem to fit this present case at all.'

'The thing that attacked Mr Holmes,' said Catherine, 'and almost killed him was no human vampire. And it wasn't a giant bat, either. It was more like a . . . well, a snake of some sort.'

'You interest me greatly. If it doesn't cause you too much pain, please tell me more. Describe exactly what you saw.'

Catherine Crosby described her ordeal at the hands of Doctor Defoe. She found it helpful to talk about it. Somehow the memory became less painful when she did so.

'If this vampire creature,' muttered Bunyan, when she had completed her tale, 'is an entirely natural creature, I wonder how the villainous Doctor Defoe explains it to his followers?'

'What do you mean?'

'Just that he seems to have the most amazing power over the thugs who obey his wishes. They are—in all probability—terrified of him. And I wonder if part of that reign of terror is because he has convinced them that these . . . "vampire serpents", to give them a name, are occult, demonic beings.'

'I suppose it's possible,' Catherine agreed. 'Many of his followers appear to be ignorant, ill educated fellows. They could easily be convinced that Defoe has control over powers that are more than human.'

'And once they believe that they will be terrified into obeying his every wish. Yet if it could be demonstrated that the "vampire killers" are mere flesh and blood, then much of his hold over them might be broken.'

'I suppose so,' said Catherine doubtfully.

'It is time for me to take some action in this matter,' said Bunyan energetically, as he leaped up from his desk, and picked up his hat and coat.

'What do you intend to do?'

'I intend to track Doctor Defoe back to his lair.'

'But when Mr Holmes rescued Dr Watson he said that Defoe had moved from his old headquarters—and they don't know where he is now.'

'True. True. But he will remain somewhere near the river, around the docks. That appears to be his natural habitat. And I intend to track him down.'

'And once you do?'

'Once I do, my dear, I shall find a way to destroy

his supply of these "vampire" creatures—hopefully in such a way that his followers realise his limitations and abandon him.'

'Is this wise, Mr Bunyan? It sounds awfully dangerous to me. Shouldn't you leave this to the police?'

'What have the police accomplished so far? Very little! I tell you my child, there are places a clergyman can go, and people he can talk to, that are closed to a policeman.'

'I suppose so,' Catherine agree slowly, her voice still filled with concern and doubt.

'Don't worry on my account,' said Bunyan, as he picked up a stout walking stick and swung it through the air once or twice. 'I can take care of myself.'

'I have decided,' said Catherine firmly, 'that if you insist on going on this foolish expedition—then I am going with you.'

'Nonsense, my dear! I will not allow you to expose yourself to danger. You will stay here with Mrs Newbigin. Besides which it is a cold, miserable night outside.'

'If you are going—I am going,' Catherine repeated as she picked up a bonnet and shawl from the hall table. 'I warn you, Mr Bunyan, that I am a very determined young woman. If you won't take me with you, then I shall simply follow you. I won't let you out of my sight.'

'It appears that I have no choice then,' said Bunyan with shrug. 'Come along then, let's be off.'

As Mr Bunyan and Mrs Crosby were catching a

cab across London, Holmes, Lestrade and myself were travelling towards the Prime Minister's residence at Number Ten Downing Street, in a coach provided by the Metropolitan Police.

'At least the reasons for the three murders are now clear,' said Holmes, as the wheels of the coach clattered nosily over cobblestones.

'I'm glad they're clear to you, Mr Holmes,' responded Lestrade, 'because they are certainly not clear to me.'

'Come now Lestrade, think the matter through. It is the cholera bacterium which provides the common thread—surely you can see that?'

'You'll have to explain, Mr Holmes.'

'Well, the Chinese sailor to begin with—where is cholera most prevalent? In the East. I have no doubt it was the Chinese seaman who carried the deadly little bottle to London for Doctor Defoe. Having done that, he knew too much—and Defoe had him killed.'

'Crosby, the banker?' I asked. 'What about him?'

'We know, Watson, from Mrs Crosby's testimony that Doctor Defoe had lodged some valuable property in the bank vault—which Crosby then refused to return to him. Undoubtedly the "property" was the box containing the glass tube of cholera bacteria. What if Crosby had opened the box, seen the glass test tube it contained and become suspicious? Remember what his clerk told you—that he was something of an amateur scientist. Crosby may have been sufficiently suspicious to refuse to return it until he had arranged for it to be analysed.'

'In which case Defoe had to kill him in order to prevent the analysis and to get the deadly little container back into his own hands,' I said.

'Precisely, Watson,' said Sherlock Holmes.

'But Mr Holmes,' interrupted Inspector Lestrade, 'what about the night watchman at the pumping station.'

'Simplicity itself,' Holmes remarked. 'Defoe had to find a way to introduce the bacteria into the city's water supply—hence he was exploring ways into the pumping station. The unfortunate night watchman happened to be in the way at the time.'

'I must admit,' Lestrade said, 'that when you explain these things Mr Holmes they seem so clear and simple. And yet I just can't see them by myself.'

18

Mr Bunyan and Mrs Crosby had their cab set them down in Narrow Street, near Victoria Wharf. Thick fog was drifting in off the river. The glow of yellow lamps, and the sound of voices, came from the pubs. Catherine stepped closer to Mr Bunyan, and slipped her hand through his arm, nervously. Bunyan himself began to wonder whether this expedition was such a wise idea after all.

'Where do we start?' Catherine asked in a nervous whisper.

'There is a friend of mine who lives not too far from here,' replied the clergyman.

'A friend?' said Catherine in surprise.

'A Salvation Army officer. He works among the slums. And he knows everyone around here. And all the gossip. This way, my dear. He lives in a tiny place down one of these back alleys. If only I can find the right one.'

They plunged into a twisting maze of narrow lanes

and alleys, all filled with the dank, heavy fog from the river, and all of them dark and narrow. After about ten minutes of taking turn after turn, Bunyan was about to admit that he was lost when a large, heavily built man stepped out of the shadows.

'Good evening grandpa. Good evening missy,' he snarled.

'What do you want my good man?' asked Bunyan.

'I want you to hand over your purse—you see, I'm not anyone's "good man". I'm not very good at all,' cackled their assailant with a vicious laugh.

'In that case,' Bunyan replied, 'although I believe strongly in charity, I think it best if I give you no money at all.'

'Oh, I'll get your money off you all right—alive or dead,' snapped the man, as he whipped a huge knife out of his pocket.

The next moment there was a blur of action, as Bunyan's walking stick whirled through the air. The man cried out in pain, and the knife clattered onto the pavement.

'Now, be off with you,' Bunyan said firmly. The man growled savagely, but turned and hurried away, clutching his wrist. 'I told you I could take care of myself,' said the clergyman to his young companion. 'Now, let's press on—we can't be too far away from Captain Redwood's place.'

Within five minutes of the attack, Mr Bunyan and Mrs Crosby were standing before a narrow, green painted door.

'This is it,' said Bunyan, as he knocked loudly.

The door was opened almost immediately by a tall, thin man in a Salvation Army uniform.

'Henry!' he cried. 'This is a pleasant surprise. Come in, come in.'

After introductions had been made, and tea had been poured, Bunyan explained the purpose of their visit.

'What exactly are you looking for?' asked Captain Redwood.

'If Doctor Defoe has relocated his headquarters recently, there must have been some movement, some suspicious activity—perhaps something going on that was kept secret, and that ordinary folk were kept away from. You know everything that happens down here, Tom—what rumours have you heard?'

'Now that you ask, over the past twelve hours I've heard people talk about a certain warehouse, down on Victoria Wharf, that no one is allowed to get close to any more. There is a band of thugs surrounding the place—very discreetly, of course. But no one is allowed to get close.'

'And which warehouse is this?' asked Catherine.

'It's called Fidden's Warehouse,' replied Redwood, 'and it's full of turpentine. You can smell the stuff as soon as you start to get close.'

'Is it hard to find?' asked Bunyan.

'I'll draw you a little sketch map, if you like,' Redwood said, 'but I'd advise against going there.'

'We are after the murderer of this young woman's husband. It is a time for boldness, Tom,' said Bunyan firmly.

A short while after this Mr Bunyan took his leave. He tried to persuade Catherine Crosby to wait for him with Captain Redwood, but she steadfastly refused, and insisted on accompanying him into the lion's den.

Meanwhile, Holmes, Lestrade and I were in the Prime Minister's study. Upon entering we were introduced to the Prime Minister, Lord Salisbury, to the Home Secretary and to the Secretary of State for War.

Then the Prime Minister handed Holmes a note, asking, 'What do you make of this, Mr Holmes? Should we take it seriously?'

Holmes read the note aloud: "Unless you wish tens of thousands of your people to die horrible deaths from cholera, you will place one million pounds in a packing case, and place the case on the edge of the Victoria Wharf. Do so before dawn or your people will begin to die. All police are to be evacuated from the Victoria Wharf area. Sherlock Holmes will assure you that I do not make idle threats. (Signed) Doctor Grimsby Defoe."

'Well, Mr Holmes,' asked Lord Salisbury. 'Should we take this matter seriously?'

'Deadly seriously. This man has the means at his disposal to carry out his threat. And he is such a thoroughly evil creature that he would not hesitate to do so.'

'Must we pay the money?' asked the politician, wringing his hands anxiously.

'If I may make a suggestion, sir,' said Inspector

Lestrade. 'Fill the packing case with old newspapers, place it on the wharf as directed, and I will surround the place with my men. We will catch this fiend when he tries to collect the money.'

'Much too dangerous,' snapped Holmes. 'This man is devious, cunning, unscrupulous and highly intelligent. To do as you suggest Inspector, would be suicide.'

'Then what do you suggest?' asked the Home Secretary.

'Do exactly as Doctor Defoe requires. I take it you can obtain the money?'

'The Chairman of the Bank of England is standing by.'

'Excellent. Then contact him. Place the money in a packing case exactly as the note says. Evacuate all police officers from the area.'

'But Mr Holmes!' cried the Secretary of State for War. 'We can't just give in to terror and blackmail.'

'You won't be giving in,' Holmes assured him. 'Dr Watson and I will be there. We are not police officers. Our presence does not violate the instructions in the note.'

'But what can two men do against such evil?'

'That,' said Sherlock Holmes quietly, 'remains to be seen.'

19

The Reverend Henry Bunyan struck a wax match against a nearby brick wall, and by its flickering flame tried to read the sketch map Captain Tom Redwood had drawn for him.

'It's no use,' he complained. 'This map doesn't make sense to me any longer. These narrow lanes twist and turn too much.'

'Just a moment, Mr Bunyan,' said Catherine Crosby. 'Can't you smell it?'

'Smell what?'

'Turpentine. I've been smelling it—faintly—for the past minute or two. And I think it's getting stronger.'

'By George! I do believe you're right.'

'So, all we need to do, Mr Bunyan, is follow our noses,' said Catherine in a whisper. 'We must be getting close now.'

The two crept slowly forward, through the dark, fog filled alleys. At each corner they stopped and sniffed, and the smell of turpentine told them which way to proceed.

Rounding a corner they came upon a bundle of dirty rags, from which came the sound of loud snoring. Bunyan examined the sleeping man closely.

'He smells of cheap gin. He is undoubted supposed to be guarding this approach to the warehouse.'

'We've been lucky then,' Catherine said.

'Or guided. Evil men despise the power of God, but it remains the greatest power of all.' As they crept cautiously forward he added, 'Hush, my dear. From here we must be as quiet as the grave.'

Catherine clutched the back of Mr Bunyan's long, black coat as the two crept silently forward. Step by step they drew closer to the back wall of the warehouse. By now the smell of turpentine was almost overpowering.

Bunyan ran his fingers lightly along the wall of the warehouse, searching in the pitch dark for a door or window. After a moment his fingers trailed over a rough wooden surface.

'A door,' he whispered to the young woman behind him. He tried the handle—it was locked.

'Let me try,' whispered Catherine. She extracted a hatpin from her bonnet, slipped it into the lock on the door, and manipulated it. Several minutes later there was a quiet click, and the door swung open at a touch. Mr Bunyan and Mrs Crosby stepped inside the warehouse that was the new lair of Doctor Defoe.

At that same moment, Holmes and I were stepping off a police launch at Ratcliffe Cross Wharf. The packing case containing the money had already been deposited at Victoria Wharf—just up river from us.

'Good luck,' said Inspector Lestrade, and shook our hands, as we stepped ashore.

'You have a revolver, Watson?' asked Holmes, as the police launch disappeared into the fog.

'Here in my pocket,' I replied.

'Keep it ready. We may need it at any moment.' So saying he led the way along the edge of the docks towards the rendezvous with Doctor Defoe.

The thick, damp fog wrapped itself around us like a living thing. In that darkness and fog we moved like two blind men, guided only by sound—the slap of the water from the river on our right, and the faint echo of our footsteps from a brick wall on our left.

'We're almost there Watson,' whispered Holmes.

'How can you tell?'

'I've been counting my footsteps and, since I know the exact length of my stride, I can calculate the distance we have walked.'

'How will we be able to see when they approach the packing case in this impenetrable gloom?'

'Because Defoe's thugs will have to strike a match or produce a small lantern to identify the case.'

'That won't help us. A dim light would only penetrate a few feet in this fog.'

'However, Watson, I arranged with Lestrade to have a phosphorescent marking painted on each side of the packing case. That will pick up even the dimmest light and glow for some minutes.'

'Most ingenious, Holmes!'

At that same moment Mr Bunyan and Mrs Crosby were creeping slowly between barrels of turpentine towards a dim light and the sound of murmuring voices. They came to a halt behind a stack of barrels, looking towards two large heavily built men who were sitting on barrels smoking cigarettes.

'Very foolish,' whispered Catherine.

'What is foolish?' asked Bunyan.

'Those two men. Smoking. So close to this highly inflammable turpentine.'

Bunyan was about to reply when his foot slid forward, and, instead of finding solid flooring, slipped over the edge of a deep cavity. He had to struggle not to lose his balance and fall in.

'What was that?' said one of the thugs, when Bunyan made this slight scuffling noise.

'Just rats again,' grumbled his companion. 'Pay no attention.' With that they turned away, and resumed smoking in silence.

'That was close,' whispered Catherine, when she was sure they were safe again.

'We must find out what is in that cavity,' Bunyan whispered in response.

The two of them lay down on the rough wooden floor of the warehouse and inched forward until their heads were peering over the deep, wide opening in the centre of the building.

At first their eyes could see nothing. But as they slowly became accustomed to the darkness they began to make out a tangle of writhing, wriggling shapes below them.

'It's the pit,' hissed Bunyan excitedly. 'The pit in which Doctor Defoe keeps his blood sucking vipers.'

'Yes, you're right,' said Catherine. 'But now that we've found them, what can we do about them?'

'The turpentine,' Bunyan whispered.

'I don't understand.'

'We open up a barrel or two of turpentine and drain the contents into the pit—very quietly, of course, so that those two guards cannot hear us.'

Together Mr Bunyan and Mrs Crosby quietly lowered one of the barrels of liquid on to its side, removed its stopper, and allowed its contents to trickle down the side of the cavity and into the pit containing the vampire serpents. Having emptied one barrel, they then did the same with two more.

They were reaching for a fourth when a dim lamplight appeared behind them and a familiar voice said, 'Well, well—what do we have here?' It was Doctor Grimsby Defoe.

20

Faintly through the fog came the sound of a steam launch moving towards the wharf. It chugged, and gurgled on low power, and then the sound ceased. A moment later there was a thump as the launch touched the timber side of the docks.

'That will be Doctor Defoe,' whispered Sherlock Holmes. 'No one else would be out on the river at this time of night, in this weather.'

Next came the sound of muffled voices, and the faint noises of ropes being tied around a bollard. A rattle of timber told us that a gangplank had been extended, and that someone was stepping ashore from the launch.

'Keep low, Watson,' whispered Holmes, 'and move slowly forward.'

A moment later a dim glow appeared through the fog. It was the phosphorescent markings Holmes had arranged to be painted on the packing case. The glow was only a few yards ahead of us. There could be no doubt now—Doctor Defoe was examining his prize.

Soon came a sharp creak, as the lid of the case was levered open with a crowbar. The evil doctor was, I assumed, checking the contents of the case. He must have been satisfied, because after several minutes the lid was hammered back into place. Echoing footsteps then crossed the wharf in the direction of the warehouse.

'What now?' I whispered in Holmes' ear.

'You wait here for Doctor Defoe to return,' he replied. 'I am going on board that launch for a few moments. I shall return shortly.' An instant later he was gone from my side. I drew the revolver out of my coat pocket, checked that it was fully loaded, and then settled down to wait—in the darkness and the fog.

At that same moment Doctor Defoe entered the warehouse, took the cover off a small lamp he was carrying and walked around the pit to check on the state of his vampire killers. As he did so he discovered, in the glow of his lamp, two intruders—the Reverend Henry Bunyan and Mrs Catherine Crosby.

'Well, well—what do we have here?' he said.

Bunyan and Catherine made no response. She looked pale and terrified, while the clergyman looked grim and determined. Before them stood the dreaded figure of Doctor Grimsby Defoe, wrapped in a long, black cape, with a broad brimmed black hat on his head, and heavy black leather gloves on his hands. His strange, green eyes were filled with hatred as he glared at them.

'Nothing to say for yourselves? In that case, I have no time to waste on you. Tie them up!' snapped the evil doctor to the thugs by his side. A few minutes later Mr Bunyan and Mrs Crosby were lying on the floor, side by side, their wrists and ankles firmly bound with stout ropes.

'We're leaving,' snarled Defoe. 'I shall return later to deal with these two, and tend to my pets. In fact, these two will make a delightful meal to keep my pets' hunger for blood satisfied.' As he spoke he gestured towards the pit that held an unknown number of his blood-sucking vipers. 'You shall remain on guard,' he continued, pointing to one of the thugs. 'The rest of you, come with me.'

One of the thugs who had been guarding the warehouse flicked his cigarette onto the floor, and marched out onto the wharf with Doctor Defoe and the others. The second guard resumed his seat, his back towards the two captives.

A minute later Mr Bunyan whispered to Catherine, 'Look!'

Startled by the urgency in his voice she glanced in the direction he indicated. She could see a small, blue flame, burning slowly but steadily across the floor—the burning cigarette had ignited a trail of spilled turpentine. And it was burning towards the pit—that was now filled with hundreds of gallons of the inflammable liquid.

'What shall we do?' she hissed. 'Alert the guard?'

'He would only flee for his life and leave us here to die,' replied Bunyan. 'To be honest, my dear, I

104

don't really know quite what to do . . .'

But before he could finish this statement he was interrupted by a cheerful, small voice.

'Never fear—Wiggins is 'ere!' it said.

'Wiggins,' gasped Catherine. 'You wonderful boy!'

'Yeah, I know I'm wonderful. Now, keep still while I cut your ropes with my pocket knife.'

'But . . . but . . . how did you manage . . .?'

'Mr Holmes told me to keep an eye on you,' explained the street urchin as he sawed through the ropes. 'I've been followin' you two ever since you left Baker Street.'

'But we saw nothing,' protested Bunyan.

'Of course not. I've been taught 'ow to follow people by the best in the business—Mr Sherlock Holmes 'imself.'

A moment later they were free. As they struggled to their feet the guard, hearing a noise turned around.

'Hey! What's going on—' he began to shout. But he stopped abruptly, because at that moment a sheet of flame burst out of the viper pit. As the flames roared, the thug turned in terror and ran. From the pit itself came the most horrible sound—a savage hissing noise as the creatures slithered over each other trying to escape the flames. The hissing rose in volume until it almost became a scream, and then it died away to be replaced, not by a noise, but by a smell—the appalling stench of burning flesh as the vampire creatures met their grisly end.

While this was going on, I was keeping my post

on the wharf. I heard a slight movement near me in the dark.

'Holmes, is that you?' I whispered. For a moment there was silence, and then two huge hands, as strong as iron, grabbed my arms.

'Disarm him, and bring him here,' called a voice across the wharf. I recognised that voice. It was Dr Grimsby Defoe. I was dragged across the timbers of the wharf into a dim circle of yellow lamp light. And once again I found myself face to face with the most evil man in London.

21

'It seems I am to be plagued by interfering fools tonight,' snarled Doctor Defoe. Clearly, the criminal mastermind was in a foul temper. 'It will make no difference to my plans. I have my reward,' he continued, reaching out and placing one black-leather gloved hand on a large packing case. 'And before the authorities can begin to search for me, I will have disappeared from the face of the earth. Tie him up and take him to the warehouse with the others.'

I was seized by those powerful hands again, but before I could be dragged away the shrill note of a policeman's whistle cut through the fog, and a sharp voice called, 'Surrender Defoe—we have you surrounded.'

Doctor Defoe stopped in his tracks. For a moment he looked uncertain, and then a dark expression passed over his face. He turned back towards me and snarled at the thug who held me, 'Kill him.' So, I thought, this was how I was to die—at the hands of a ruffian, on the instructions of a man who was evil incarnate. I caught one glimpse of the man who had been ordered to execute me. There was a smile of wicked pleasure on his face.

I saw the flash of a knife, then heard the explosion of a gunshot, and saw my would-be killer drop dead at my feet. At that same moment the warehouse behind us exploded in a sheet of flame. A wave of searing heat swept over us. The darkness was lit by a blaze of burning red and yellow light as the fire turned night into day along the length of the wharf. Looking around I saw Doctor Defoe turn and run towards his launch.

'Cast off you fools!' he shouted as he ran, all thought of the packing case and the money it contained forgotten. 'Quickly! Quickly!'

The sound of the launch engine could be heard as steam hissed through the cylinders. Defoe leaped into the vessel just as it pulled away from the wharf.

As the launch moved off towards the middle of the river, into the thick fog, Defoe shouted across the waves, 'You have defeated me this time Sherlock Holmes—but you haven't caught me! I shall have my revenge.'

Why is he blaming Holmes? I wondered. It was the police who brought about his undoing. At that moment Holmes was by my side.

'Where are Lestrade's men?' I asked. 'These thugs need to be rounded up.'

'There are no policemen, Watson,' said Holmes

calmly, 'only me and my trusty police whistle.'

'And it was you . . .?' I began to ask.

'It was indeed me who shot your attacker, Watson.'

'Holmes, you've saved my life! How can I ever . . .'

'Think nothing of it, old fellow.'

At that moment Wiggins appeared, leading two rather singed, scorched and smoky looking individuals—the Reverend Henry Bunyan and Mrs Catherine Crosby.

'What on earth . . .?' I stuttered. 'I don't understand.'

'It's a long story, Dr Watson,' said Mr Bunyan. 'I'll explain it all later.'

'Just a moment,' I cried in alarm. 'What about the bottle of cholera bacteria? Defoe still has it. And now that he has been defeated he will use it. Thousands will die.'

'This Watson,' said Holmes quietly, holding up a small, glass bottle, 'is the bacteria that evil mastermind used to threaten London.'

'How did you obtain it?'

'I was certain that Defoe would have it close by tonight. I was right. While he was in the warehouse, I slipped aboard the launch and found it. Unfortunately, just after I took this container, I was discovered by one of Defoe's thugs and had to flee. As I did so, the bottle of nitroglycerine I was carrying in my pocket fell onto the deck. I was most fortunate that it did not explode as it fell. I fear that it may explode at any . . .'

Before the words had left Holmes' mouth a mammoth explosion shattered the night. The very air seemed to rock with the force of that volcanic charge. Small pieces of the timber hull of a boat rained down upon us, as our ears continued to ring painfully.

'And that,' said Mr Bunyan, 'is, I believe, the end of Doctor Defoe.'

It was over breakfast the next morning that I finally learned everything that had happened. Seated around our table in Baker Street were Catherine Crosby, Henry Bunyan, Inspector Lestrade, and even young Wiggins, in addition to Holmes and myself.

'A most satisfactory solution,' muttered Lestrade, his mouth half full of hot, buttered toast. 'The money has been recovered and is safely back in the Bank of England. The cholera bacteria has been handed over to the chief chemist at St Bartholomew's Hospital. Those vampire creatures appear to have been completely destroyed in the fire at Fiddens' Warehouse. And, perhaps best of all, the evil Doctor Defoe will trouble us no more.'

'Tell me, Mr Bunyan,' said Catherine Crosby, 'how can one man be so unspeakably wicked?'

'Human nature, my dear,' replied the clergyman. 'We like to think that someone as evil as Doctor Defoe is completely different to us—that he is basically bad and we are basically good. Not so, I'm afraid. There is a shadow of corruption on the human heart—and Dr Defoe just shows us how black that shadow can be.'

'What sort of "corruption"?' Catherine asked.

'Selfishness, pride, self-importance—that's what it is my dear. Those things are natural—because human nature is corrupt. The word the Bible uses is "sin". The word "sin" has "I" in the middle. I sin when I do what I want—without thinking about God. The truth is, we have all behaved badly because we have all ignored God—and by ignoring Him we have hurt ourselves and hurt other people. We are all guilty of that. Defoe simply took our experience to its darkest extreme—he simply did as he liked, regardless of how much he hurt God or other people. That is why all of us—not just the Doctor Defoes of this world—need to turn back to God, turn from living our way to living His way.'

'Of course there was one thing that Doctor Defoe didn't count on,' interrupted Inspector Lestrade.

'And what is that?' asked Catherine.

'That we had on our side—Mr Sherlock Holmes!'

**Sherlock Holmes and Dr Watson
will return in**

The Loch Ness Monster

Watch out for it!

A Note from the desk of Kel Richards

In "*The Adventure of the Golden Prince-Nez*" by Sir Arthur Conan Doyle, Dr Watson refers to "the repulsive story of the red leech and the terrible death of Crosby the banker" but nowhere does he record the details of that story.

In this book I have supplied the details that Dr Watson omitted—and I hope I have made them "repulsive" and "terrible" enough to please you!

I have also drawn on an idea from another of the great storytellers—H G Wells (author of *The Time Machine* and *The War of the Worlds*) by taking up an idea he suggested in his short story "*The Stolen Bacillus*" which is set in the same time and place as this book—the foggy London of 1895.

Remember that your suggestions for future Sherlock Holmes adventures are always welcome (the more mysterious and spooky the better!).

Next in this series, Holmes and Watson chase spies and sea serpents in the adventure of *The Loch Ness Monster*—don't miss it!

Best wishes (and good detecting!),

Kel Richards

SHERLOCK HOLMES' TALES OF TERROR

A preview of what's next from

Kel Richards

THE LOCH NESS MONSTER

7

As the fishermen ran towards their boats moored at the town jetty, Holmes and I volunteered to join the search party. We ended up in the same boat as the two Taggarts—father and daughter.

Donald Taggart and I pulled on the oars, while Holmes took up a watching position in the stern of the boat, and young Sarah did the same in the bow. The fishing boats spread out in a broad pattern across the width of the Loch—slowly moving towards the western end.

We had not rowed far when a cold, white mist began to rise from the surface of the inky, black water. I was glad to be rowing, for the exercise kept me warm, and counteracted the chilling influence of the cold, white fingers of mist that lifted themselves from the Loch and seemed to wrap themselves around us.

Before long the mist was so thick we could not see the other boats.

'Does the mist always rise as quickly as this on Loch Ness?' asked Sherlock Holmes.

'Aye, that it does, Mr Holmes,' grunted Donald

Taggart as he pulled on his oar. 'You have to have a good sense of direction to be a fisherman on this Loch.'

As we rowed we could hear the voices of the other fishermen in the other boats as they called, 'Robbie! Robbie! Can you hear us? Where are you lad?'

But the other boats were all invisible in the spreading, thickening mist, and the disembodied voices floated across the water like the cries of lost souls.

'This Robbie Stevenson who has gone missing,' began Holmes.

'The water bailiff? Aye, what about him?' said Taggart.

'How well did he know these waters?'

'He knew the Loch as well as any man living, Mr Holmes.'

'Then he couldn't have got lost? Or been taken by surprise by the weather conditions?'

'Oh, the Loch can take anyone by surprise, sir,' grunted the fisherman, as he continued rowing. 'Loch Ness can be dead calm at one moment, and filled with waves that can smash your boat to pieces half an hour later. It's the Great Glen, you see—it acts like a funnel in the way it tunnels the wind down onto the water.'

'Stop your rowing,' shouted Sarah from the bow of the boat. 'There's something ahead in the water.'

Taggart and I rested our oars in the water and let the boat drift. A moment later Sarah said, 'It's only some matted weed floating on the surface. You might as well start rowing again.' Her voice sounded disappointed—and worried.

The voices of the other searchers became fainter and fainter as they spread out across the Loch. 'Robbie! Robbie, lad, can you hear us?' they shouted—dim voices from invisible people lost in the deep, white mist that filled the air and filled our lungs, and chilled us to the very bones.

'How can you be sure we won't get lost in this wretched mist?' I grunted between strokes on my oar.

'I can't be,' admitted the fisherman beside me. 'But I have a fair idea of where we are.'

'Pa's being modest,' said his daughter loyally. 'He has the best sense of direction of any fisherman on the Loch.'

'What was that?' snapped Holmes urgently.

'Your ears are sharper than mine, Holmes,' I said. 'I can't hear a thing.'

'Listen!' he said.

Taggart and I stopped rowing, rested on our oars and listened.

'There it is again!' insisted Holmes.

'I didn't hear a thing,' I admitted.

'Quiet. Listen,' said the fisherman beside me.

The four of us sat very still, as the boat slowly rocked up and down on the gentle swell. Somehow the heavy mist seemed to have deadened our sense of hearing as well as our sense of sight. Then the sound came again—and this time I heard it.

It was a deep throated cry. Perhaps more like a rumble than a cry.

'Have you heard that sound before, Mr Taggart?' asked Holmes.

'Aye, sir, that I have. And I don't like it at all.' His voice was trembling as he spoke.

'It's the water kelpies,' whispered Sarah Taggart quietly.

Then it came again. This time it was a deep throated roar—and there was no avoiding the note of menace in that sound.

There could be no doubt about it: there was an animal, a very large animal, somewhere in the waters of Loch Ness—and it was not very far away from us.

At that moment, in a small, secret boatshed, at the far western end of the Loch, a meeting was going on that was to have a profound impact upon us before too long.

The man who had been spying on us from the peak of Dun Dearduil was meeting with one of his confederates.

'Is it now fully active?'

'As far as I can tell, it is,' replied the short, nervous man who was with him.

'Can you control it?'

'Only very slightly. It will respond to certain sounds and certain smells—but not always.'

'Can you make it more aggressive?' asked the rat-faced man, with the thick, black beard.

'We can use the high-pitched underwater whistle that we trained it with.'

'What effect will that have?'

'I can't be sure. But if we use it repeatedly it might become more agitated, more active, and more likely to attack.'

'Then try it. We must speed this process up.'

'Yes, sir.'

I was to learn of that deadly planning meeting only much later. While it was going on, I was out in a small fishing boat on Loch Ness with Sherlock Holmes, and Donald and Sarah Taggart, listening to a savage animal, whose roar echoed across the waves towards us.

'What is it?' asked Holmes, in his quiet, calm voice.

'It is the creature,' replied Taggart, his voice little more than a murmur.

'What creature?' I asked, feeling alarmed.

'The creature of the Loch. What Sarah called the "water kelpie". Very few folk have heard its cry and lived to tell the tale.'

Just then its roar came again—but this time it was further away, and growing fainter as we listened.

'It's leaving us,' gasped Sarah, in a hopeful whisper.

The next roar was little more than a dim echo from some great distance across the water. 'Yes, child, you're right,' muttered Donald Taggart. 'God has taken mercy upon our souls.'

'Upon our bodies, more likely,' I said. 'If that thing has teeth to match its roar, I wouldn't fancy meeting it up close.'

Further discussion of what we had heard was prevented by Sarah's sudden cry of alarm, 'Wreckage ahead—in the water.'

Once again the fisherman and I lifted our oars and let the boat drift. A moment later we heard the clunk of something solid hitting the side of the boat. With some difficulty Sarah pulled it out of the water.

Holmes clambered forward to examine what she had found.

'This is part of a boat,' he said. 'It's certainly no ordinary driftwood. Start rowing again—but slowly.'

Over the next ten minutes we found a dozen small pieces which were all that was left of a timber rowing boat. Then something soft thudded against the side of our craft. Holmes leaned forward over the gunwale to look at it, then he said, 'Sarah, you had better go to the seat in the stern of the boat, while I pull this body on board.'

Sarah did as she was told, then Holmes, Donald Taggart, and I pulled on board the soaking wet body that was all that was left of the missing man.

'Is this Robbie Stevenson?' asked Holmes.

'Aye—that's him. Or what's left of him,' affirmed Taggart.

'What killed him, Watson?' Holmes asked, turning towards me.

I knelt down in the boat and conducted a cursory examination.

'Impossible to say,' I responded after a few minutes. 'The body has been too badly mangled to be able to tell.'

SHERLOCK HOLMES' TALES OF TERROR

What lurks beneath the black waters of Loch Ness?

The top-secret submarine is being tested in Scotland's Loch Ness.

Sherlock Holmes—the world's greatest detective—has been called in to investigate.

But can any of them escape from the monster that lurks beneath the inky black waters of Loch Ness?

The local fisherman are terrified. Young Sarah Taggart warns them of the dangers to be found in those dark waters.

Will Sherlock Holmes and Dr Watson survive when they come face to face with the beast beneath the Loch?

THE LOCH NESS MONSTER

#4

Coming to a bookstore near you!

KEL RICHARDS

SHERLOCK HOLMES' TALES OF TERROR

THE CURSE OF THE PHARAOHS

Something strange is walking in the darkness! Professor Soames Coffin has spent his life studying the secrets of ancient Egypt—and as he lies, dying, in his dark, old mansion in Scotland he believes the old magic of the Pharaohs will bring him back to life. Soon the creature who is The Walking Dead is stalking the living . . . including Sherlock Holmes!

KEL RICHARDS

SHERLOCK HOLMES' TALES OF TERROR

THE HEADLESS MONK

The ghost is after the gold! The legend from the Dark Ages has come to life—the monk that has no head—and it's hunting for the missing treasure of 40,000 gold coins. A terrified lighthouse keeper and his family call upon Sherlock Holmes—the world's greatest detective—to protect them from deadly danger.

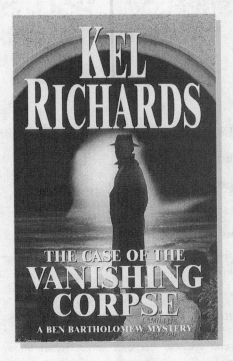

The world of Ben Bartholomew is a world of standover gangs and armed terrorists, a world in which a private eye for hire must carry a gun if he wants to live beyond lunchtime. When Ben Bartholomew begins investigating, he finds that he has stumbled onto the ultimate locked-room mystery!

Guaranteed to be a can't-put-down book.